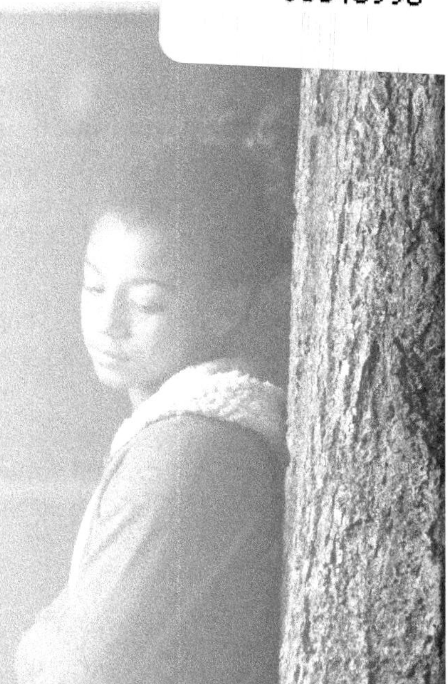

In Keisha's Shadow

Sandra Barret

Bedazzled Ink Publishing Company * Fairfield, California

978-1-934452-83-7 paperback
978-1-934452-84-4 ebook

2nd revised edition
First published 2009

Cover art
by
TreeHouse Studio

Nuance Books
a division of
Bedazzled Ink Publishing Company
Fairfield, California
http://nuancebooks.bedazzledink.com/

Dedicated to Walter Haddock, cancer victim, and Caryl Haddock, cancer survivor.

Ovarian Cancer – know the signs, break the silence.

ACKNOWLEDGMENTS

Sincere gratitude to the folks who helped me beat this story into readable shape, including Kimiko Koopman, the psychocommagrlz critique group, and Carrie Tierney, my intrepid and patient editor. Special thanks to Shula, the wife, for her horse expertise, and in general, for putting up with me.

Chapter 1

TORI KAHL IGNORED herself in the dog-eared arcade instant photo and stared at the blond girl whose arm was draped over her shoulder. Her ex-girlfriend's sparkling blue eyes stared back at her. She hated moping over the picture again, but old habits die hard, and after three months, this one wasn't going to die at all.

First love sucked.

The voice from hell echoed down the hallway outside Tori's bedroom door. She slipped the photo of her and Robyn back into her overstuffed leather wallet just as her mother appeared in the doorway with a towel wrapped around her straightened black hair.

"Get a move on. And why are you still using that pathetic wallet? I gave you a perfectly good purse for your eighteenth birthday."

"Keisha was your purse-carrying daughter, not me." Tori stepped past her mother and shut her bedroom door. Bringing up her half-sister's name in the past tense still stung, but it was worth it to see her mother's reaction. A full minute passed before her mother regained the ability to bitch, plenty of time for Tori to pop into the upstairs bathroom, splash some water on her black, corkscrew curls, and finger comb them back into shape.

"You're going to be late for your first day at college."

Tori tuned out her mother's nag as she bounded down the stairs, rounded the bend in the hallway, and skid into the kitchen to grab lunch. Her younger brother, Jerome, kept his eyes glued to the laptop at the breakfast table.

"Can I get a ride down the hill with you?" Jerome scratched his fingers through his wavy brown hair as he read whatever was on his laptop.

She envied him for looking more like their Jewish father. Why did she have to be the one to inherit their mother's African American hair?

"You can't walk the mile to St. James Academy?" She stuffed two mini blueberry muffins into her mouth.

"I could walk, but then I'd miss your charming company," he said.

Tori cuffed the back of his head before she grabbed an apple and granola bar for lunch.

Her mother clicked into the kitchen in heels. She clasped a black leather notepad under her arm while simultaneously adjusting an earring and glaring at Tori. "You should have left by now."

"I am." Tori swung her purple backpack over her shoulder. "Come on nerd-boy, let's go."

Jerome closed his laptop at the last moment and stuffed it and his homework into his backpack.

She did not envy him his last two years at St. James. If it weren't for Robyn's help, she'd have failed her last year there. She didn't want to think about Robyn because that brought up memories of being dumped right outside Keisha's funeral.

The whole summer sucked.

She got into the driver's seat of her dirty blue Ford Focus and started the engine. Jerome slid into the passenger seat. She pulled out of the driveway and drove down the winding, wooded road that led from their Santa Cruz mountain home to Santa Clara. Two minutes later, she stopped in front of the stone and iron gates of St. James Academy.

A wisp of cool air rushed into the car as Jerome opened his door. "Thanks." He slammed the door shut and trotted up the private road to his school.

Tori turned back onto the main road and sped down the hill. She lowered the windows to let the cool air swirl around her, stirring the tight curls of her hair. Within two miles, she saw the brown haze that hovered over Santa Clara Valley. It would be a warm September day with no hint of the fog layer that kept her mountain home cool.

Twenty minutes later, she found what she thought must be the last available parking spot at De Anza College and made her way across her new college campus with her backpack full of textbooks for the day. She ignored the cluster of students jammed into the campus bookstore. Thanks to her mother's nagging, she'd purchased her books three days ago.

"Tori! Hey, Tori!"

Tori turned back toward the bookstore and scanned the crowd of students. She caught sight of a small face surrounded by a black-haired ponytail and square-framed glasses.

"Jackie!" She hoisted the backpack higher onto her shoulder and weaved her way through the crowd to her friend.

"Long time no see. What's it been, a week?" Jackie's dark, Asian eyes glanced up at Tori as she led the way out of the crowd and back into the open air.

"More like two days. Where's your squirrel-chasing boyfriend?" Tori dropped her backpack on a patch of grass and joined it on the ground.

Jackie sat beside her, folded her legs up, and dug into her own backpack. She pulled out a soda, cracked it open, and offered Tori the first sip.

"Thanks." Tori took a long gulp and handed the soda back to Jackie.

"Matt came on campus last week to get his books. You know what he's like," Jackie said. "He's probably read through all of English Lit by now and half that massive history book. What's your schedule like?"

Tori didn't mention coming early for her books. That would be admitting she'd let her mother win an argument. Instead, she dug out her schedule. "I've got History with you and Matt on Tuesdays and Thursdays, Math for dummies after that, and Psychology every day but Fridays."

"Sounds like a blast." Jackie put her soda on a level patch of grass. "Have you heard from you know who?"

"No." She hated the slight shake in her voice. "Robyn was pretty clear she was through with me back in June."

A frown pushed Jackie's glasses further down her small nose. "She's such a bitch."

"If I had any guts at all, I'd have come out to my mother, and Robyn wouldn't have left me."

"Come out at your sister's funeral? I don't think so." Jackie grabbed Tori's arm. "Just because Robyn's the Queen of Out doesn't mean you have to be. Any sane person would realize that would have been the worst timing in the world."

Tori wrapped her arms around her knees, trying not to remember Keisha's funeral but failing. Keisha's father had been there and all their mother's black relatives. Tori barely knew most of them since their mother had moved south when she married Tori's father. Tori had always been closer to her father's side of the family. "Robyn was trying to be supportive."

"In front of all those praise-Jesus Baptists? You know Robyn would have been all over you like white on rice."

"Brown rice," Tori said with a weak smile.

"She was already full swing on her out and proud mission. Not letting her come to the funeral was the smart thing to do."

That didn't lessen the sting from the nasty phone breakup they'd had right outside the funeral home. Tori pulled a pearl-handled pocket knife out of her back pocket and started twiddling with it between her fingers.

Jackie closed her hand over Tori's, stopping her. "I have something better." She pulled a plastic water bottle out of her backpack and handed it to Tori with a wink. "Don't say I don't look after you."

"Thanks."

The "water" was vodka, compliments of Jackie's older brother who made sure she had easy access to liquor. He charged extra, but it was a hell of a lot easier than trying to fool a cashier into thinking she was of legal drinking age. Tori pocketed her knife and dug out some money to pay Jackie. The vodka would shut her mind up for a little while.

"What are you doing after classes?" Jackie asked.

"I'm off to the horse stables. I have seven stalls to muck out."

Jackie finished off her soda. "Shoveling horse shit. Doesn't that sound exciting?"

"It pays Saxon's boarding bill. And it's better than waiting around for squirrel-boy."

"Matt better meet me after my last class, or I'll hitch a ride home with one of these other guys." Jackie scanned the crowd around them as if she was seriously thinking of replacing Matt, but Tori didn't believe it. It had been Jackie and Matt since the start of high school. It would always be Jackie and Matt.

She hoisted her backpack off the ground as she stood. "My class is on the other side of campus. See you tomorrow in History." She waved goodbye and bolted off across the campus to her first college class. Outside the classroom, she drank some of the vodka. She'd save the rest for later.

TORI DROVE INTO the late afternoon sun, wishing she could find her sunglasses. She turned into Shadow Oaks Stables. The hard-packed dirt road rattled under her tires. A pair of horses played in the turn-out area on her right. One of the horses belonged to Michelle Chomsky, the barn manager. That meant Michelle was around somewhere.

Tori parked her car in the shade of a scraggly oak tree, stirring up more dust than necessary after an ungraceful stop. She kicked off her shoes and stuffed her feet into a worn pair of formerly-tan work boots that were covered in a layer of dried mud. The round training pen was empty so she trotted down the tree-lined path to get her horse out for exercise. Saxon whinnied his greetings as she went inside his stable. She slipped his halter around his thick, black neck. After picking the caked dirt out of his hooves, she led him to the round pen.

While Saxon trotted a wide circle around the pen, Tori scanned the outer pastures, searching for Michelle. She saw her stooped over a broken section of the mares' pasture. Michelle's unmistakable red hair glowed in the warm late-summer sunlight. Tori cut Saxon's exercise short and tied him to a post with some hay to eat.

She trudged up the hill to Michelle. "What happened this time?" She lifted the other end of a weathered two-by-six plank that Michelle was hammering back in place.

"Ruby." Michelle hammered in the last nail on her side. "I don't know what she sees in these fields of dry weed, but she kicked out a couple of planks and escaped again."

"Where'd you find her?" Tori accepted the hammer from Michelle and nailed her end of the plank to the thicker corner post.

"Outside the hay barn, eating the bits that fell off the feed truck."

Tori laughed. Ruby was Michelle's twelve-year-old chestnut mare who assumed she had the right to search out food when the mood struck. Combined with a typical volatile mare's temperament, Ruby was a hard horse to keep in line. Tori was glad she owned a gelding.

They walked down to the round pen. Ruby stood near the side, respecting the metal fencing. Tori verified that Saxon still had hay to munch on and then followed Michelle into the round pen.

"Do you want to help train Marcus?" Michelle picked up a whip and encouraged Ruby into an easy trot.

"Sure." Tori crouched between the bars of the fence and circled around to the small set of stables behind the pen. She grabbed a halter for Marcus, the buckskin yearling that Michelle was training. He couldn't be ridden for another two years, but once trained, his unusual coloring guaranteed an easy sale.

Marcus stomped impatiently as she looped the lead rope over his neck to hold him still while she tied the rope halter on his head. She led him out of the stable and into the pen. He barged his way past her when she swung open the gate.

She grabbed the lead rope at the end and let him trot and buck out his excess energy at a safer distance. When he settled, she walked him to the center of the arena.

"Has he been a pushy boy?" Michelle asked in a teasing voice. "Let me show you how to make him respect your space."

Tori listened as Michelle taught her and Marcus together. It was the highlight of her time at the stables. She didn't resist her wild imagination when it came to Michelle, either. It was a way to forget Robyn for a while.

With Marcus behaving better, Michelle let him off the lead rope to run free. Ruby kept the younger horse in line with a sharp kick to the side when he tried to bite her. Tori occasionally shook the whip to keep the horses trotting along the outside edge of the round pen.

"Are you up for a Togo's run?" Michelle slowed the horses down and handed Marcus's halter over to Tori.

"Sure." Tori stabled Marcus and Saxon while Michelle returned Ruby to the repaired pasture. She hopped in the passenger side of Michelle's white pickup truck for the five minute drive to the sandwich shop.

She hopped down from the high truck seat and walked into Togo's after Michelle. She tried to keep her eyes off of Michelle's well-shaped waist and concentrated on the menu displayed above the counter. After their sandwiches were ready, they slid into a booth by the front of the shop overlooking the parking lot.

"So how was your weekend?" Tori asked before taking a big bite of her meatball sandwich.

"Busy. I roped Joel into helping me repair a stable roof. He says I owe him big for it."

Tori didn't like hearing about Michelle's boyfriend. It was stupid to fantasize about a straight woman anyway. She changed the subject. "Are we doing a Halloween horse show this year?"

"I was thinking about just a fun costume show or something."

"And a jump course?"

"Of course."

Tori couldn't jump Saxon in a western saddle, but she jumped bareback well enough to beat most English riders.

On the ride back to the stables, Michelle convinced Tori to set up all the decorations, get the gifts and ribbons, and print out a flyer to announce the Halloween show. Michelle had a way of getting her to volunteer for a lot more than she'd planned for. At least she had over month to prepare.

A KNOCK ON Tori's bedroom door interrupted her online reading. She minimized the browser window that pointed to her favorite lesbian fan fiction site.

"What?" she asked, hoping the heat in her cheeks subsided before she faced anyone.

"Do you have to keep this locked?" her mother asked through the closed door. "You still haven't washed the pots from dinner."

Tori opened the door. Her mother was dressed in tight-fitting workout clothes. Her dark brown skin glistened with a sheen of sweat. *Straight from the treadmill in her den*, Tori thought.

"I'm taking a shower. I want those pots done when I get out."

Tori stepped into the hallway and shut her door. She avoided her mother as she headed down to the kitchen. Her brother sat in the family room watching TV, and there was no sign of her father yet. She half-heartedly started washing the pots in the large steel kitchen sink. When she heard the sound of the shower running upstairs, she dried her hands on her pants and opened the kitchen cupboard. A half-finished bottle of single-malt whiskey sat in the back of the top shelf. She took three fast swigs from the bottle before putting it back. The initial shock of the whiskey's strong taste warmed her chest.

She returned to the sink and finished off the pots. With her mother still upstairs, she managed one more gulp of alcohol before leaving the kitchen and locking herself back in her room. She returned to the middle of the steamy love scene she'd been reading.

A half-hour later, her bedroom floor rattled as the garage door beneath her opened. Her father was home. She debated going down to say hello. Of course, she risked bumping into her mother again, but she was feeling pretty good now. After shutting down her computer, she skipped down the stairs in time to meet her father by the side door. He put his "Kahl Veterinary Clinic" hat on the coat rack and dropped his work case by the door.

"Another emergency?" She watched her father from the base of the stairs.

"Foster's mare gave birth tonight." Ed Kahl ran a hand through what was left of his faded blond hair as he walked into the living room. His frame filled the doorway, making him look more like a trucker than the owner of a large animal veterinary clinic—the clinic he hoped she'd work at if she went to vet school after college.

Of course, her mother reminded her that if she didn't apply herself, she'd never survive four years of college, never mind veterinary school. Good thing there wasn't a test for motherhood and nurturing. Her mother never would have passed.

She heard the footsteps on the stairs as she plopped down next to her father on the beige sofa. Jerome mumbled about them interrupting his television time. Tori's mother entered the room, her damp hair wrapped in a towel again. She'd traded workout clothes for a pair of tan slacks and short-sleeved blue blouse.

"So, was it a colt or a filly?" Tori asked.

Her mother joined them on the sofa, briefly interrupting Jerome's view of the television as she walked by. Her father sat with one broad arm around Tori's shoulder and the other around his wife's.

"A fine looking palomino colt."

"Did you take any pictures?" Tori asked.

"Of course. I'll upload them from the camera this weekend for your collection."

"You mean her shrine." Jerome gave up and turned off the television.

"Better than your shrine to all things geek," Tori said.

"Anyway," her mother said. "Were there any complications?"

"No. It was an easy delivery."

Her mother snorted. "Only a man could call a delivery easy."

"So, Tori, how was your day?" he asked.

"Pretty easy. I just picked up the reading assignments and the schedule for the quarter from each class."

Her mother leaned over to glare at her. "Don't cut classes like you did in high school. They'll drop you from the class, you know."

"Yes, I know."

"Well," her father said, breaking the tension, "I'm exhausted. I'm going to take a shower and go to bed." His deep blue eyes crinkled as he grinned and ruffled Tori's corkscrew curls. Somehow, it always made her feel special. "I know you'll do well."

Her parents left together.

"Movie or video game?" Jerome asked.

"Video game. I haven't roasted your backside with a flamethrower in at least a week."

TORI WOKE UP the next morning with a dull headache. Two Advil and a can of Coke later, her day should have picked up, but it didn't. Her mother had taken the morning off and roped Tori into her plans. They stood in the upstairs hallway with the late summer sun heating up the bedroom that wasn't Tori's or Jerome's.

"You can step inside the room, you know. It's not like her ghost is going to come bite you in the backside."

She glared at her mother from the doorway to Keisha's

room. The specialized hospital bed still looked out of place, even after being a part of the room for months before Keisha died. The bureau was the same as it had always been, though, and the nightstand where Tori had stolen the pearl-handled knife she kept in her pocket. "Why do we have to do this now?"

Her mother squatted down at the edge of the bed, studying the frame. "Because the hospice people have someone who needs this kind of hospital bed, and it makes no sense for us to keep it here anymore. Now help me figure out how to take it apart so we can get it downstairs."

"Why don't you wait for Dad and Jerome?"

Her mother stood back up. "Because you're here now. Keisha was your sister, too, so get your butt in here and help me."

"Fine." She hated being in this room. She'd hated it from the moment Keisha was diagnosed with an aggressive form of cervical cancer and had to move back home to live in it. And die in it. Not that it mattered, because Tori had no way to get out of helping move the bed. "What tools do you need?"

It took them two sweaty hours to separate the rails from the bed frame, take the frame apart, and move it into the garage where the hospice people could get it the next day. By the time they finished, Tori's thoughts were a tangled mess of memories from the last months of Keisha's life. As soon as she could, she locked herself in her own bedroom and stripped to boxers and a tank top to cool off.

Tears weren't her thing. Screaming and putting her fist through a wall was her thing, but her mother would have a fit if she did that again. She pulled the knife out of her pocket and flicked it open. When she'd stolen it, the blade had been dull, but now it held a perfect edge, sharp and clean.

Her first cut across her thigh didn't sting right away. By the third cut, she was going deep enough to feel nothing but the pain in her leg. It was better that way, the physical pain over the mental. She looked at the marks on her leg, red from the new, bleeding cuts, crossing over the white scar lines of an earlier episode. She could play tic tac toe if she tried. Should she immortalize a win for X, O, or a draw?

Chapter 2

TORI'S CAR KICKED up a cloud of dust as she pulled under the oak tree and parked. A family of five, most leasing Michelle's horses, stood to the side of the tie up as Michelle saddled their horses.

"Sorry," Tori whispered to her as she took the next horse from the sand holding pen and tied it to a post.

Michelle greeted her with a relieved smile. "Overslept?"

She gave a noncommittal shrug. She wasn't going to admit that yesterday's activity had sent her into a tailspin, and she'd forgotten all about the trail ride.

"I'm getting you a new alarm clock." Michelle tightened the girth on her horse.

Tori scrambled to saddle the last horse and Saxon, ignoring the stinging cuts in her thigh. Michelle matched horse to rider based on the experience level of each member of the waiting family. Tori rode Saxon up as Michelle helped the youngest family member into the saddle.

"I'll be in front," Michelle said. "You ride in back and keep them from straggling too far apart. The kids have all taken lessons so it's only the parents I'm worried about."

Michelle hopped on Ruby. She led them up beyond the mares' pasture and into the adjacent county park land. The wide trail, shadowed from the sun by overhanging scrub oak, wound up along the outer rim of the Santa Cruz Mountains. They passed the next set of trees to see a clear view of the south bay and peninsula. Michelle paused to take pictures of the family on horseback with the bay as backdrop.

"Pretty good showmanship," Tori teased, feeling more like herself as she waited for the picture taking to end.

"Impress the riders, and they come back again," Michelle said with a wink.

When photo time ended, Tori returned to her spot at the rear. They took a meandering trail past the water towers and along the outskirts of an active stone quarry. The other side of the quarry wasn't far from her house. Before she got a car, she used to cut across the quarry and down these trails on her bike.

After an hour and a half of trail riding, the family looked ready to be back on their own feet. Michelle led them to the stables and settled the bill, while Tori untacked the horses.

Michelle came back and handed her forty dollars. "What did you think of being a trail guide?"

Tori pocketed the money. "The pay's good." She unbuckled Saxon's bridle and replaced it with his rope halter.

"Are you interested in another next weekend? I've got a group of six coming."

"Sure." She walked Saxon to the wash rack and hosed off his sweaty patches from the saddle. The mother from the ride ran up from the parking lot just as she finished scraping off the excess water.

"Sorry," the mother said. "Can we get a picture of our trail guides?"

Michelle laughed. "Sure thing."

Michelle wrapped her arm over Tori's shoulder and pulled her closer. Tori held her breath, frustrated by the flush in her cheeks from Michelle's closeness. The instant the picture was taken, she stepped away and took Saxon back to his stable.

She groomed her horse until her emotions settled down. She wouldn't crush on Michelle. The woman was straight, involved, and old, at least thirty. Tori locked up her tack room and walked the dusty trail back to her car. She heard Michelle's rolling laughter from inside one of the stables and ignored the way it made her stomach do flip-flops.

"SO WHO'S COMING into this stable?" Tori hoisted her end of a dirty mat while Michelle lifted the other end. The movement disturbed patches of old horse urine. Tori coughed, wishing she had a free hand to block her nose. "When's the last time anyone cleaned these mats?"

"Try never. The new boarders are coming in this afternoon." With another hearty shove, they folded the mat over, releasing another wave of stench that brought tears to Michelle's eyes. "I was supposed to clean this up for them last week but there was too much else to do. Thanks for the help."

"No problem." Tori looped a rope through the fold in the long mat. Together, they pulled it all the way to the cleaning rack.

Tori hosed it down and kicked off the caked clumps of dirt and manure. Michelle took the stinky job of scraping ages of old manure from the stable's exposed dirt floor. The mat was just as heavy when they dragged it back, but at least the stable had aired out some. They were both exhausted and smelly by the time a truck with a trailer rattled up the dirt road behind them.

"That's the new boarders." Michelle brushed her chest and stomach, but didn't remove much of the dirt caked to her clothes.

Tori caught herself staring at Michelle's efforts and focused instead on the newcomers. A large grey pickup truck pulled an older model two-horse trailer into the parking lot. All she could see was the swish of a tail inside the trailer. Michelle walked up to the front of the truck, but Tori held back, not really interested in whoever the new people were. She sat on the wood picnic table and kicked some of the excess dirt off her boots. When she looked back at the group, her gaze trailed from beautiful black eyes down a firm body to well-shaped legs.

"She's beautiful." Tori walked toward the group as if in a dream. Coming to her senses when she stood next to Michelle, she flushed in embarrassment.

"Gorgeous, isn't she?" Michelle said.

"Yeah." Tori stroked the grey-white body of the most gorgeous Arab mare she'd ever seen. "What's her name?"

A deep voice spoke up from behind her. "Tank Girl."

Tori forced herself to look away from the horse to greet an older man with thick gray hair and a scruffy beard who stepped up from behind the trailer. "You have a beautiful horse."

"Not mine, my granddaughter's," he said. "I'm Iain Metcalf. That's my granddaughter, Ashley, leading our other horse to the turnout."

Tori saw a heavyset brown-haired woman about her own age. She led a chestnut gelding into the temporary paddock where it would stay until it was ready to join the other geldings out in pasture. "What's your other horse's name?"

"Apostle. He's a ten-year-old quarter horse draft mix." Iain's voice held the hint of an accent she couldn't quite place.

"Cool. How old is Tank Girl?"

Ashley walked up beside her to take Tank Girl's reins. "She just turned three this summer. Michelle's going to train her." She held out a well-tanned hand. "I'm Ashley."

Tori shook the offered hand and mumbled her own name then backed away to let her take Tank Girl to the stable they'd just cleaned. She'd never been present when Michelle saddle-trained a young horse. Maybe she'd get to help.

"Tori, can you bring Buckwheat and Buddy down and put them in the turnout with Apostle?" Michelle asked. "We need to get him used to the horses he'll be joining in pasture."

"I'll help you with that," Iain said.

Tori walked away with Iain, disappointed that she wasn't able to listen in while Michelle explained her training plan with Ashley.

"How long have you been riding?" Iain asked.

"Since I was about ten. My neighbor had an old gelding that I took out for walks. When nobody was around, I'd hop on his back for a ride. They said he was too old but he loved it."

He smiled as he walked beside her. "I know the feeling. Everyone's ready to put us old folks out to pasture whether we've still got some kick left in us or not."

She picked up a piece of bale twine and rolled it in a ball to keep any horses from eating it. "When did you start riding?"

"I started when Ashley did, when she was eight. It's one of the few things she still lets me do with her. I don't suppose you'd understand how much parents miss their children when they drift away, eh?"

She couldn't imagine her mother missing her for any reason, but her dad might. They still shared a love for horses. That's why she clung to the ridiculous notion of becoming a vet some day. Not that she had the grades or motivation for that much schooling.

"We bought Apostle about four years ago, then Tank Girl last year so Ashley could train her own hunter-jumper horse."

"Do you compete?" She grabbed Buddy's lead rope and halter and passed it to Iain. She took up Buckwheat's halter and rope and looped it over her shoulder while she opened the metal gate to the gelding pasture.

"No, not me. I like trail riding mostly, but since we share Apostle, I've learned a few dressage tricks. How about you?"

Sean Connery, that's who he sounded like. He had the same hint of a Scottish accent. Tori scanned the pasture, looking for the two horses they'd come for. "I compete in Western shows. I like barrel racing. We're organizing a fun show for Halloween in two weeks, with costumes and games. You should come."

"That's Ashley's territory. I'm sure she'll want to enter with Apostle."

Tori pointed out Buddy and then went off to gather Buckwheat. She had farther to walk to get her horse, so Iain was already back at the turnout with Buddy loose by the time she got there. Michelle and Ashley were no longer in sight.

She let Buckwheat loose. "I'm going to head off. I'll see you next time."

"It was nice to meet you," Iain said. "I don't ride as much these days, but I'm sure you and Ashley will see each other quite often."

She said good-bye to Iain and walked back to her car.

Michelle wouldn't start training for a few days anyway, to give Tank Girl time to get used to her new home. Tori would make sure she was around when that training started.

TORI LISTENED TO the radio as she pushed the clutter around in the back of her closet. Somewhere in the mess were her history notes from high school. They had to be better than the pathetic notes she'd taken so far in her college class. She shifted her old comic books and saw the grey binder of her history notes peeking out from under a box. A tug on the binder toppled the box on top of it. A stack of lavender paper spilled out.

She jumped up and locked her bedroom door, then rushed back to the closet. If her mother found Robyn's letters, she'd be toast.

Tori unfolded the top letter. She shouldn't wallow in old memories, but the temptation was too much. Robyn had teased her, joked with her, and all but made love to her through these notes. She used to stuff them in Tori's locker, in her school-books, and sometimes in her pockets. Text messages and e-mails were too obvious for Robyn. She liked the challenge of making Tori find her hidden notes.

> Hey T,
> Movies tonight? Mom said it's okay for you to stay
> over . . .

Tori folded the paper and stuffed it back in the box as the memories came rushing back. The letter hadn't been her first invitation to spend the night with Robyn, but it was the last. Two weeks later Keisha had died and so had Tori's first relationship.

She shoved the box deep into the back of her closet and shut the door. She should toss all the letters, burn them some night when everyone was out. Her clock radio said it was just past midnight. Everyone else in the house was asleep. She pulled a sweatshirt over her pajamas and snuck out of her room.

In the kitchen, she mixed Kool-Aid into a bottle filled two-thirds with water. After listening for a moment to be sure no one else was up, she slipped inside the den and closed the door. She opened a bottle of rum, topped off her Kool-Aid, and returned the bottle. Just as silently as she'd come down, she went back up to her bedroom with her drink.

The next morning, Tori awoke to the sound of her brother pounding on her bedroom door. A lead weight had replaced her head some time in the night, and she felt it when she rolled over to eyeball the clock. It was past seven o'clock. She closed her eyes and let her throbbing head fall back onto the pillow. It seemed just an instant later that her mother's voice hollered through her locked bedroom door. Tori jumped out of bed in response and landed on the floor in a clump of bed sheets.

Cursing, she stood up, slower this time. The clock showed 7:45 am. With a groan, she kicked through her dirty laundry, finding the least messy clothes. She stumbled into the bathroom for a shower. Four Advil and a gallon of water later, she was almost ready to face the day. She grabbed the empty water bottle from her room and filled it with soapy water in the bathroom sink to remove any lingering odor of rum.

Her mother was drinking her coffee in the kitchen. "What's the sense of an alarm clock if you never set it properly?"

"Why set it if I'm going to sleep through it anyway?" Tori bypassed the coffee machine and pulled a soda out of the fridge. Her mother raised one eyebrow but didn't say anything. They'd already had the argument that Coke was no worse than coffee in the morning.

"You look a mess." Her mother rinsed out her coffee mug and stuffed it into the dishwasher. "There are frozen waffles in the garage freezer if you want any."

Tori's stomach did a back flip. "No thanks."

"Are you feeling all right?" Her mother picked up her briefcase and turned to Tori one last time.

Tori held up a hand and stood. "I'm fine. I'm late for school." She downed the rest of her soda and stuck the can in the recycle bin. Her mother watched her as she made her way back upstairs but by the time she got back down, the house was empty. She grabbed her backpack and headed off to a history exam she wasn't prepared for.

THE INSTANT TORI pulled into the stable parking lot, she knew her visit was ruined already. Apostle and two other geldings took up the turnout area. Michelle and Ashley were in the round pen with Tank Girl. They were busy with the lessons she hadn't managed to weasel her way into yet. That left no place to exercise Saxon. She parked her car and walked to her stable, ignoring the stab of jealousy she felt when Michelle didn't even stop to wave at her from the arena.

She wouldn't let the sunny day go to waste. After picking the dirt out of Saxon's hooves, she saddled him up for a ride. With no one else around to ride with, she headed up the hill to the open dressage arena to work on fast stops and turns.

After forty-five minutes, both she and her horse were sweaty even in the cool October breeze. She rode back to the wash rack in a far better mood and tied Saxon up. She turned the hose on herself, soaked her hair, and let the water drip down her front and back.

"Nice place for a shower." Ashley sat on a bench by the wash rack, watching her.

Tori turned off the hose. "It beats being sweaty." She shook the excess water out of her curly hair.

"I wish I had your hair." Ashley looped a strand of her shoulder-length straight brown hair behind an ear as she bent over and drank from the still-dripping hose.

"Yeah, right." Who would want to replace silky straight hair with the tangled curly mess that sat atop her head?

Ashley wiped the water from her lips. "I'm serious." She toyed with Tori's wet curls. "They're cute."

Tori took a step back. "How's the training going?"

Ashley gave her a mischievous smile before sitting back on the bench. "Pretty good. Tank Girl's trotting well enough with a saddle strapped on, but she still bucks like mad when we first let her loose. Michelle thinks it will be another week or two before anyone can get on her."

Tori looked around. "Where is Michelle?"

"She's gone off to buy us some lunch."

The ugly twinge of jealousy returned. Not that she expected Michelle to spend more time with her than Ashley. After all, Ashley was paying Michelle to train Tank Girl.

"You're welcome to hang around for lunch," Ashley said. "I'm willing to share."

Ashley's grin made her feel like an open book when it came to Michelle. "No thanks. I have a lot to do." Like studying so she wouldn't fail another history test.

"I heard you're organizing the Halloween show. Is it too late to enter?"

"Anyone who shows up can enter. Probably nothing like what you're used to."

"That's okay. It'll still be fun to enter with Apostle. Especially the jumping events."

She tried to judge what kind of competition Ashley would be at the show. Ashley was overweight, so that was to Tori's advantage, but she hadn't seen her ride yet, and Apostle certainly looked fit. It could be a challenge.

"How much longer is Apostle going to be in turnout?" she asked.

"He goes out to pasture in a couple of days. It'll be a pain to have to catch him in pasture before I ride. You're lucky to have yours in a stable."

Tori didn't mention how much work she did around the barn to offset the cost of Saxon's boarding. She heard Michelle's voice and turned in time to see her waving to them as she approached.

"Hey, Tori. I could have picked you up a sandwich too but

I couldn't find you." Michelle joined Ashley on the bench and placed a large Togo's sandwich bag between them.

"That's okay. I need to get going anyway." It was a lie, but she didn't want to watch Ashley flirting with Michelle.

On the way to the car, she flicked on her cell phone and called home. If everyone was out, she'd have easy access to liquor.

"YOU'RE JEALOUS," JACKIE said.

"What? No, I'm not." Tori pulled out a notebook from her backpack, placed it on the classroom table, and pretended to read.

Jackie reached over and flipped it shut. "You are so jealous. I know you, Tori Kahl. And that's your jealous face."

She pulled her notebook out of Jackie's reach. "What the hell is a jealous face?"

Jackie leaned on the table. "You get all squinty-eyed. I've seen it before."

"Well, I'm not jealous now. If Michelle prefers to spend all her time with some chubby English rider and her fancy new horse, so what?"

"Uh-uh. Nope. That's not jealous."

She leaned past Jackie to poke Matt in the shoulder. "Can't you control your girlfriend?"

The gangly redhead looked up from the book he was reading. "Huh? What?"

"Never mind." For the first time, ever, she wished history class would start on time. She was not jealous of Ashley and Michelle.

"So how fat is this new girl?" Jackie asked.

"Huh? Ashley? I didn't say she was fat."

"Chubby?"

"Well, she's big, you know. For a show rider." She felt a twinge of guilt for picking on Ashley, but she was dominating most of Michelle's free time, and she was flirting with Michelle. A lot.

Jackie stared at her. "You mean she's not stick thin like the rest of the pre-pubescent girls who go to horse shows."

"Hey. I'm not stick thin or pre-pubescent." Tori stuck out her sizable chest to prove it.

"No, but not every girl can be blessed with not so much as an ounce of body fat like you. As a lesbian, I'd have thought you'd be more accepting of the varieties of women's bodies."

"I am."

"So am I." Matt's green eyes lit up.

That earned him a smack on the shoulder from Jackie. "Yeah, you both sound it. When was the last time someone described a woman as Rubenesque and you thought, oh, sexy?"

Tori stifled a laugh. "When was the last time anyone called a woman Rubenesque, period? Not all of us are art-major wanna-bes."

"Funny, ha, ha. Who would have thought that a lesbian could be sexist?" Jackie crossed her arms.

She didn't get a chance to respond as their history teacher entered the room with a stack of graded exams under her arm. She didn't care if Ashley was heavy. She crossed her own arms and frowned. It didn't matter. She wasn't jealous because she didn't get crushes on straight women. Michelle was definitely straight, and too bad if Ashley was too thick to figure that out on her own.

An hour and a half later, Matt ran off to his next class, while she and Jackie walked toward the cafeteria. She crumpled the exam and tossed it in the first trash can she found. The sunny day didn't seem so sunny to her anymore—not with her second D in History. Her mother's voice echoed in her mind, harping once again on what a waste Tori was and how she'd never get anywhere in life. She didn't have Robyn around to bail her out anymore. No more study sessions that actually involved studying.

No more study sessions that didn't involve studying either. Tori needed a distraction. They walked past the bookstore, lined with a row of free magazines and newspapers outside the door, and she grabbed one.

"'The Job Finder'?" Jackie asked as they settled at a table outside the cafeteria.

"I need money." She pushed her backpack under the table and started flipping through the newspaper.

Jackie read over her shoulder. "'Work from home. Earn over $1000 a month.' You don't believe that hype, do you?"

"No." Tori flipped the pages faster, but most of the ads were similar money-making schemes. Hawking someone's trash wasn't the kind of job she'd be good at. Flipping burgers was more her speed. She slapped the last page down and sunk her head to the table. "It's October already. The stores must be hiring for the Christmas rush."

"Why the big push for money? I thought your parents were paying for college."

Tori lifted her head. "That's the problem. If I don't get top grades like Keisha did, they'll make my life hell. Maybe if I made enough money, I could pay my own tuition." Maybe even move out. Then her mother would have to hunt her down to bitch her out. That was more effort than the shrew would expend on her behalf. She knew getting a job and making enough money was a pipe dream, but it gave her something to focus on besides her dismal history grade and her inability to let go of the girl who dumped her.

Chapter 3

TORI AND MICHELLE sat at the picnic table at the barn, organizing ribbons and small prizes for the Halloween horse show the next day. Tori's stack of prizes didn't match the stack next to Michelle, but she didn't have quite the same knack for pansy girlie-work. She tied a black and orange bow on the first prize package. "How many people have signed up for tomorrow?"

"Fifteen so far. We'll probably have some of the stable boarders drop in for different events."

A pickup truck rumbled up the dirt path. Tori swallowed her frustration when she recognized Ashley's truck. She concentrated on filling the prize bags with Halloween candy, but couldn't avoid noticing Ashley. The deliberate sway in Ashley's hips told her that she knew she was being watched and was making a show of it.

"Mind if I lend a hand?" Ashley squeezed herself between Tori and Michelle. Her words were mild enough, but Tori saw the look in her eye and recognized the double meaning. Ashley seemed to have a one-track mind. She'd flirted with her and Michelle at the same time. She even flirted with Jen, a horse owner Tori couldn't stand.

Michelle gave Ashley a stack of award ribbons and a list of events. "You can write the event type on these."

Ashley scribbled on the awards. "I'll be turning Apostle into a leopard." She nudged Tori. "Did you get your costume ready?"

Tori didn't bother to hide her effort to move away from Ashley. "I've got long black capes for me and Saxon. And I painted my old boots silver."

"What are you going to be?" Michelle asked.

"A black rider from *Lord of the Rings*."

"Sexy," Ashley said with a wink.

Tori ignored her comment. She wanted to skip out for the afternoon, but Michelle was paying her to prepare the upper arena for the Halloween contests. Having Ashley there bugged her, so she rushed through her stack of prizes. "I'm going to drag the arena. I'll see you later."

She hopped on Michelle's feed tractor and drove up the hill. A rusted chain harrow lay beside the sand arena. She attached it to the back of the tractor and drove around the arena. The harrow dragged the sand smooth, eliminating the hoof marks and divots from training lessons. When she finished, she checked all the jump poles and lined them up at the edge of the arena. The jump competition would be the best event.

Michelle was gone, and Ashley was riding Apostle in a slow trot in the round pen by the time Tori drove back down. She walked away from most of the stables, but still within view of Ashley in the round pen, and pulled out one of Jackie's special soda bottles. The first sip told her it was coconut rum mixed with Coke this time. She leaned against a tree to study her riding competition for tomorrow.

The relaxation that came with liquor filled Tori's senses as she watched Ashley practicing jumps. For all that Ashley got on her nerves, the girl had talent. Not enough to win, but at least Tori would have someone to compete against.

Time slipped by as she enjoyed her drink. Ashley packed up and left, not realizing she'd been watched the whole time. Ashley was okay, when she wasn't talking, flirting, or, in general, anywhere nearby.

Tori needed to get home as well. She shouldn't drive right after drinking, but she hopped in her car and took off anyway. Her road seemed extra twisty in the dim light, but she managed to make it home without any incidents other than screeching her tires when she slammed the brakes too hard in the parking lot.

TORI DIDN'T HEAR her alarm clock go off at six-thirty Saturday morning. She didn't hear her father leave at six forty-five. What she did hear was her mother pounding on her door at six fifty-five.

She rolled over and squinted at her clock. She still had over an hour to get to the horse show, but her mother wasn't going to let her fall back asleep.

"Never should have told her I need to be somewhere this morning," Tori mumbled as she dragged herself out of bed. She pulled on her least-dirty pair of jeans and a wrinkled but clean men's work shirt with the name "Eddie" stitched over her right breast. After stopping just long enough to use the toilet, she was down at the breakfast table within five minutes.

That wasn't fast enough for her mother, who glared at her across the table. "You're eighteen. When are you going to start being responsible for yourself?"

Her mother stood between her and the fridge, and Tori recognized the onset of another lecture. She wouldn't be allowed to eat until her mother ran out of steam. She pulled out a chair and settled in for the duration.

"At your age, your sister was already hitting the pavement, looking for an internship."

Tori picked up a paperclip and straightened it. "Keisha didn't look very far."

"What's that supposed to mean?"

"You hired her." She couldn't help it. Winding up her mother was like an Olympic event. Her mother's quick intake of breath meant Tori was looking at a bronze medal already.

"Of course we hired her. She showed all the passion and dedication you lack."

Tori took the tip of the paperclip and started scratching the names she wanted to call her mother into the palm of her hand. If she didn't push for the silver or gold medal, maybe she'd have time for breakfast before getting the hell out of the house.

"You're not setting appropriate goals for yourself. Your father and I agree that something has to be done."

Her palm scratching started to bleed at the edges, but the sting wasn't as bothersome as her mother's voice. "Browbeat Dad into submission again?"

"Tori Kahl! That's enough!"

Tori glanced up. Bulging eyes, and her mother used her full name. Silver medal achieved.

"Look at yourself. You look like a boy, you get your clothes from second-hand shops, and have you even touched your hair this morning."

Tori made the mistake of running a hand through her hair on instinct, the hand she'd been digging at with the paperclip.

Her mother was at her side in a flash. "Good, Lord. What have you done to your hand?" She grabbed Tori's wrist and pulled it forward, revealing a series of little bleeding scratches across the palm.

Tori hadn't realized how much she'd been poking at it while her mother blabbed on. She pulled her wrist back and curled her hand into a fist to cover the marks. "I have to go or I'll be late for the show."

Her mother managed to stuff gauze and some tape into the open window of the car before Tori pulled out of the driveway. She didn't say anything else as Tori drove off, but the worried expression on her face ruined Tori's chance of keeping her silver medal for Olympic Parent Harassing. Worried suggested caring, and that just didn't fit in Tori's world, not from her mother anyway. She ignored the gauze for the entire drive down the hill, but she'd need it to hold her horse's reins later. It irked her that her mother knew that.

Forty minutes later, she was riding Saxon in small circles around the lower training arena, getting him used to the feel of the black cape draped over his back and withers. Her gauze-covered cuts stung every time she gripped the reins. A nagging voice in her head that sounded just like her mother's said she'd lose the competition because of it. She hated that voice.

Ashley and Iain were already at the top arena for the costume competition when Tori rode up. Apostle's leopard spots looked pretty good, but the best costume was Jen's paint horse dressed like a cow, complete with udders.

Michelle stepped out from the little booth where she'd set up all the prize ribbons. "Thanks everyone for coming. For the costume competition, I'd like all the riders to start around the arena in a walk."

Tori pulled into the line behind Ashley. She expected a smart remark, but Ashley wasn't paying attention to anything, including the competition. She rode with her head down, letting Apostle follow Jen's cow-painted horse around the square arena.

"Is this too early for you?" Tori asked. She got a middle finger for an answer. And she thought *she* was grumpy in the morning.

Michelle called for all the horses to change direction. In mid turn, Saxon's cape stuck in his hind hoof, startling him into a trot. Apostle flattened his ears, but stayed in line as Saxon trotted past. Tori reined him into a tight circle, ignoring the cuts stinging her hand, then rejoined the parade.

"Riders, form a line, please." Michelle stepped into the booth and came out with a handful of ribbons. The riders positioned their horses in a line, each horse facing Michelle. "Fifth prize goes to Tori and her dark rider."

Tori bent down to accept the last place consolation ribbon. She rode Saxon out of the arena, followed by the fourth and third prize winners. Ashley took second prize and Jen's cow costume took first prize.

"The haunted pony race is next, in ten minutes," Michelle said. "Each rider gallops around the arena with one of these dragging behind them." She rattled a life-sized plastic skeleton in her outstretched hand.

Tori stripped off her cloak and Saxon's cloak and exchanged her painted silver boots for her normal tan work boots. She eyed her competition, knowing none of the regulars could match her and Saxon, but then she saw Ashley trotting in a tight circle to warm Apostle up. Ashley had changed into a navy riding jacket over a white blouse and tan breeches stuffed into black riding boots. The outfit suited her, but more importantly, she rode well. Tori knew who she'd be competing against for the rest of the show.

She and Saxon were the third to compete. When Michelle dropped the flag, they took off at a smooth canter. The plastic skeleton rattled behind them as they neared the first barrel and turned. Saxon's neck was high and tense.

"Easy now." She loosened up on the reins, ignoring the pain in her hand as they rounded the second barrel and headed for the long diagonal stretch to the finish. They stopped at the edge of the arena, and one of the younger riders ran to detach the skeleton from Saxon's saddle.

"How'd I do?" she asked.

"Fifteen-point-nine seconds." Michelle gave her the thumbs up.

Tori walked Saxon to the side of the arena while Ashley moved into position as the next rider. The skeleton hung behind Apostle, but the horse didn't budge.

Jen walked up next to Tori. "I don't think she can do it."

"Apostle looks ready to go."

"She's an English rider. That might make her good at dressage, but she'll never make the turns."

"She rides in hunter-jumper competitions, not dressage. She can cut a turn."

The flag dropped. Ashley and her horse took off at a steady canter to the first barrel and then made the first turn with ease. Tori stood in her stirrups, watching them approach the second barrel and again, swing around it without a problem. It was a fast, straight run to the finish. Michelle looked at her stopwatch and then gave Ashley the same thumbs up signal she'd given Tori.

"She didn't make it."

Tori looked down at Jen. "How do you know?"

Jen held up her own watch. "Sixteen seconds."

Jen's unofficial time didn't match Michelle's stopwatch. Tori took second prize, and Ashley congratulated her as she went to get her first prize ribbon.

Beginner competitions took up rest of the morning. She led Saxon to the upper turnout pasture, took off his saddle and bridle, and let him loose. After hauling her saddle back to her tack room, she mucked out his empty paddock and the other horses she was responsible for. She couldn't jump in a Western saddle, so she dug out her bareback riding pad.

After lunch, she returned to the arena for the last event of the day, the jump course that Michelle had designed. Tori had the bad luck of going first and had just enough time to strap the bareback pad on Saxon before it was her time to start. At the signal from Michelle, she took the first two jumps with ease. She wasn't prepared for the sharp turn to the third jump. Saxon's back hooves clicked against the top pole, but it didn't drop. She wouldn't lose points for that.

She settled Saxon down at the end of the course as she suffered through Jen's caustic comments about the skills of each rider while they watched the rest of the competition by the sidelines.

Ashley pulled her long hair back into a ponytail and rammed her head into her riding helmet. She looked far more focused than Tori had been. She'd be prepared for that third jump.

"She won't beat you," Jen said, following Tori's gaze.

"Why not?" Tori watched Iain give Ashley a leg up onto Apostle.

"She's got too much excess weight."

Tori turned to look down at Jen, who was standing beside her and Saxon. "She's not that fat."

"She's definitely stodgy."

Jackie's comments replayed in Tori's mind, but excess weight or not, Ashley was intent and ready to ride. When Michelle gave the signal to start, Ashley and Apostle took off. Apostle's gait was even, his rhythmic canter taking them through the jumps without faltering. At the end of the ride, Tori walked Saxon over to congratulate her.

Ashley smiled. "Thanks, but I don't think it was fast enough to beat your time. I can't believe you can do all that without a saddle."

Tori hid her embarrassment by turning back to the arena. Ashley's flirting was gone, and in its place was a quiet, almost humble attitude. Tori wasn't sure how to react to that.

Michelle returned her attention to the jump. "We've got a tie for first place between Ashley and Tori. We'll settle it with a jump-off."

Tori met Ashley's eyes, and her competitive edge returned. "Think you can handle jumping ever-higher rails until one of us fails?"

"I think I can take on one Western rat."

"Okay, but when I win, you owe me a soda."

Ashley walked Apostle in a wide circle around her. "Lemon-lime Snapple." She trotted toward the arena. "That's what you'll owe me when I win."

Tori followed her to the edge of the arena. Ashley wasn't so bad when she wasn't trying to get into somebody's pants.

The arena was ready, with one two-pole jump set up in the middle.

"Whenever you are ready, girls," Michelle said.

Order didn't matter, but Tori waved Ashley on for the first jump. She cleared it easily as did Tori after her. They raised the pole and jumped again. It took three rounds before Ashley and Apostle showed signs of strain. Tori looked at the poles. They were higher than she'd ever jumped before, but she could handle it.

Ashley went first again, and looked like she would clear the jump until Apostle's hind hoof banged against the top pole, and it dropped. She trotted around in a wide circle as someone replaced the pole.

"Good luck," she said as she passed Tori.

Tori had to clear the height herself or it would remain a tie. She stretched her legs, and then tapped Saxon's side with her heels. He moved into a slow canter, then pulled to the side. She veered to the left of the jump, bypassing it the first time.

She ignored the silence around her and circled again. She urged him into a faster canter, centering him in the middle of the jump. They rose over the post and landed smoothly on the other side. She turned back, just to be sure, and saw the jump intact behind her.

She won.

She hopped off Saxon to give him a breather.

Ashley had stripped off her jacket. Her white show blouse had the top two buttons undone, revealing the curve of her abundant cleavage. She took Tori by surprise when she wrapped her in a quick hug. "Congrats. So what'll it be?"

"Um, what?" Tori's brain took a moment to function again.

"The soda I owe you. Are you a Coke or Pepsi kind of girl?"

"Coke." She knew her cheeks were flushed. "Bummer about Apostle dragging his back legs."

"It fits with everything else that's gone wrong lately." Ashley retrieved her jacket and helmet. "Can you give me a leg up?"

Tori obliged, cupping her hands and supporting Ashley as she got back on Apostle. She'd never been this close to her. A trace of cologne was mixed in with the smell of horse and sweat. Tori wouldn't have pegged Ashley as a men's cologne wearer, but it definitely wasn't a lady's perfume.

"Thanks." Ashley backed Apostle up and trotted him down the hill to the stables.

Tori hopped on Saxon's back and followed. By the time she finished rinsing off his sweat and stabling him, a group of riders had already left for the Easy Jack restaurant for dinner. She and Michelle were the last two to arrive at the restaurant.

Ashley gave her a wave from across the table before she walked off on some errand.

"The waitress already took our drink orders, but she'll be back," Iain said, as Tori sat down between him and Michelle. "Congratulations on the last jump."

"Thanks."

"Ashley's heart wasn't in it today." He patted Tori's shoulder. "I'm sorry, I don't mean to diminish your win. I'm just worried about my granddaughter. Kids don't share most of their problems with their parents, do they?"

Not at all, in Tori's case. She gave a noncommittal grunt. Whatever hang-up Ashley had, it was making her a better person to be around.

The menu doubled as a placemat and she scanned it for her dinner options. Burgers and fries were an obvious choice, but the grilled cheese sounded good and was cheaper, perfect for her limited budget. Someone approached behind and tapped her shoulder. She turned to give her dinner and drink order.

Ashley smiled down at her with intense brown eyes. "I owed you one Coke."

She mumbled her thanks and accepted the glass, embarrassed to be the only one at the table to have a drink yet. She watched Ashley return to her seat.

Michelle tugged her sleeve. "What was that all about?"

"Just a private bet from the jump competition."

Michelle accepted the answer and turned to Ashley. "What are you going to school for?"

"Anthropology, eventually."

Tori's exasperated sigh came out louder than she intended.

Ashley's eyes were on her again. "Something wrong with Anthro?"

She shrugged. "It's History with a fancy name, and History's not my favorite subject this quarter."

"Anthropology is much more interesting, but I can understand hating the mandatory history class. Some teachers make it dull as dirt, but History's really fascinating with the right teacher."

Throughout dinner, Ashley's smile faded in and out. She was quieter than normal, even bypassing a couple of perfect opportunities to twist a sexual innuendo into someone else's words. Tori caught her eye once, and Ashley smiled back, but it didn't last. Ashley was in her own world, and not even her grandfather could drag her out of it.

After dinner, Tori had better things to think about. Her

parents would be at her brother's school band concert. She stopped off at her favorite convenience store, the one that didn't give a rat's ass who they sold beer to. With a six-pack in the trunk, she drove the rest of the way home to the empty house.

Chapter 4

TORI MUNCHED ON an apple while she waited. Jackie was with a dozen other students in need of a caffeine fix at the shop across from De Anza College. If Jackie didn't hurry up, they'd get caught in the first rain of the season.

"Where's your boyfriend today?" Tori asked when Jackie arrived with a hot latte in hand.

"I wish I knew." Jackie popped open her lid and blew on her drink.

"Something wrong?"

"No, I guess not. I'm just being paranoid."

"About?"

Jackie took her first sip and swore. "Do they have to make it so hot?"

Tori patted her shoulder. "Earth to Jackie. What gives?"

"Matt's just been pretty scarce lately." Jackie sipped her latte more cautiously as they began walking again.

"And that has you worried?"

"Yeah." Jackie sighed. "No. I don't know. I know he's not telling me something, you know?"

"It's probably nothing." At least, it'd better be nothing, or his squirrel-chasing days were over. "Think it'll rain today?"

Jackie looked up at the gray clouds. "Not this early in November. We've got another couple of weeks before the serious rain." As if to spite her words, a series of fat raindrops spattered the sidewalk. "Now that's just mean." She glared at the cloud that hung overhead, then covered her head with her book bag and trotted to the nearest building. Tori followed, not caring whether the rain came or not.

By noon, Jackie's mood had lifted, partly due to Matt's presence, and partly due to the results of the mid-terms she'd received. Tori's mood sank in the opposite direction. Her math and psychology scores were okay, but history was another matter. Why couldn't she have parents like Jackie's, the never around, don't give a shit what you do parents?

Matt threw an arm around her shoulder. "Who needs history anyway?"

"Me, if I don't want my mother going off the deep end." What were the chances that her mother would stop scrutinizing her grades now that she was in college?

"You'll do better on the next exam," he said.

"Sure you will," Jackie said, digging in her backpack. She pulled out a Coke bottle. "Until then, this ought to cheer you up."

Matt glared at her. "Do you have to be a walking liquor cabinet all the time?"

"Do you have to be sober all the time?" Jackie handed the rum and Coke to Tori.

She paid for it, trying to ignore the bad moment Matt and Jackie were sharing in front of her. It wasn't that Matt didn't drink, but he'd been overprotective of her since Keisha's funeral and the breakup with Robyn. He'd warned her that drinking alone was one of the signs of alcoholism. She'd gone without for weeks and never felt anything but the lack of buzz. She was killing brain cells, but she wasn't addicted.

"I've got shit to shovel," she said, opting to escape the tension between her two friends. She patted Matt on the back. "You worry too much. I'm fine."

As she drove off campus, more fat droplets of rain spattered on her windshield. She hadn't repaired the rips in Saxon's waterproof blanket. He'd spend the first rainy day of the season getting wet. Within ten minutes, the ground beneath her tires transitioned from pavement to gravel and then compacted dirt as she drove onto the barn property. She saw a few recognizable cars, including Ashley's truck, but no sign of Michelle.

TORI DODGED THE shavings Ashley heaved into a wheelbarrow outside Tank Girl's stall. She stopped short of saying hello when Ashley dropped her rake and threw up in the wheelbarrow.

"Son of a bitch! It's called morning sickness, not all frigging day long sickness."

More information than Tori needed to hear, but she couldn't escape without saying something. "Are you okay?"

Ashley wiped a grubby hand across her face, avoiding eye contact with her. "I'm fine."

Tori pulled a bottle of water out of her backpack, real water this time. "Do you need a rinse and spit?"

Ashley nodded, brushing a sleeve across her eyes. She rinsed her mouth out and passed the bottle back to Tori. "Thanks."

"It's okay, you keep it. I hear you're supposed to drink gallons of water in your condition."

Ashley winced. "How much did you hear?"

"Nothing. I mean, just the hurl and the cursing. Nothing before that. I wasn't eavesdropping or anything."

Tori's words came out in such a rush, Ashley laughed. That was a good sign, right, that Ashley could laugh at her situation?

"You don't look so good," Tori said.

Ashley glared at her. "You'd look like shit too if you were knocked up by a loser, puking your guts out for over a week and didn't have the balls to tell anyone about it or know what the hell you were going to do about it."

Tori opened and closed her mouth twice before she figured out what to say next. "I guess congratulations aren't what you want to hear right now." *Walk away.* She didn't need to deal with Ashley's emotional rollercoaster ride. Before she could think of an appropriate escape, Ashley's mood flipped again.

Eyes wide, Ashley grabbed her shirtsleeve. "Don't tell anyone, please?"

"Not going to be a problem." Talking about Ashley to pretty much anyone was the last thing on her mind.

Ashley let go as tears formed in the corners of her eyes. Her horse came into the stable to investigate the commotion.

Tori shuffled from foot to foot. She wasn't heartless enough to leave Ashley when she was on the verge of tears. "I haven't checked the pastures yet for Michelle. Do you want to take a walk?"

"In the rain?" Ashley rubbed her eyes with dirty hands.

"It's not that bad." She stepped into the pathway between the stables. "See? Barely sprinkling now."

"Okay." Ashley buried her face in Tank Girl's neck for a moment and then stepped out of the stable.

Ashley walked beside Tori, occasionally masking a sniffle as they headed up to the pastures. Tori tried to figure out how to cheer up a virtual stranger, while not getting involved in a messy situation.

She paused at the water tap outside the mares' pasture. "Did you want to, um, splash some water on your face?"

Ashley's red-rimmed eyes widened. "Am I a mess?"

"Not really. Just a little streaky, here and here." Tori pointed to her cheeks and chin.

Ashley turned on the hose and splashed cold water across her face and hands, rinsing off the mud and who knew what else. "Better?"

Thick, dark eyebrows curved over brown red-rimmed eyes, as water droplets trailed down her cheeks.

"Much."

"Sorry. I'm not usually this pathetic."

Tori picked up a discarded length of twine and balled it up. "It's okay." She gave her best sympathetic nod. Not that she wanted to hear about Ashley's man troubles, but she couldn't exactly extricate herself from the conversation now. "How long have you been seeing each other?"

"Who? Oh, you mean this." Ashley poked at her belly. "It was one night of dull sex with an even duller freshman."

They walked past the mares' pasture, and Tori made a show of checking the water trough as they continued. "What are you going to do?"

Ashley leaned against a tree as Tori wound up the water hose near the bucket. Tori glanced at Ashley, hoping tears weren't forming in her eyes again. How could she relate to someone who was pregnant? It was about as far from her future as becoming a nun.

Tears flowed freely down Ashley's cheeks as she sobbed quietly. Awkwardly, Tori patted Ashley's shoulder. "It'll be all right."

Ashley brushed her hand away. "No, it won't. I'm eighteen and pregnant. It's all downhill from here."

Tori scrambled for something else to say. "Does your grandfather know?"

Ashley paled, shaking her head. "You can't tell him about this."

"You're an adult. Why would he care?"

"He'd go crazy if I got an abortion," Ashley mumbled.

Tori leaned against the wooden pasture fence. "Oh."

"Oh."

Silence surrounded them. She never had to face the fear of an unwanted pregnancy, so she never considered abortion on a personal level. Would she abort a baby? At what point would she think of what was growing inside her as a baby versus a collection of cells?

This wasn't her body or her problem. She gazed into Ashley's eyes and saw a reflection of her own debate raging inside her, at a deeper, personal level. "Have you made up your mind?"

"No. I don't even know if I can get an abortion."

"How far along are you?" she asked. "You don't look like you're past the first three months."

Ashley sighed. "No, I'm not. I meant I don't know if I can go through with it. Getting an abortion. It's complicated."

"I'm the worst person to talk to about this, but I'm pretty sure you've got a couple of months to figure things out."

Ashley nodded.

"Maybe the test was wrong?"

Ashley laughed. "I took four different tests. Plus the whole throwing up the entire time thing."

Tori pushed off the fence. "Well, you've got time to figure it out anyway. Maybe you should give yourself the rest of the day off to just relax?"

"I still have to pull Apostle out of pasture and give him some exercise."

Finally, something she could be helpful with. "Let's turn him and Buddy out in the arena together and get them trotting for a bit."

"Thanks, that would be great."

She grinned stupidly at the smile that curved Ashley's lips. She shouldn't be so happy about lifting Ashley's spirits, but she was.

Buddy proved more difficult to catch in pasture than Apostle, cantering out of Tori's reach until she managed to coax him with a clump of hay. She looped his halter on and led him to the round pen where Ashley was already working Apostle. Ashley gave her an embarrassed smile as she let Buddy loose and joined her in the center of the pen. She let Ashley control the groundwork lesson, watching her direct both horses in a trot and then canter. Ashley had a strong focus whenever she was in charge of her horse. Her baggy jeans trailed through the mud in the arena and pulled across her round backside while she walked.

Tori shook her head. Wasn't there some unwritten rule that bi women were trouble? Pregnant bi women must be twice the trouble at least.

The gray clouds overhead opened up into a steady rain. Ashley called an end to the lesson, and they led the horses back to pasture. Tori struggled for something to say, but most of what came to mind were lame platitudes of sympathy for Ashley's state.

Ashley finally broke the silence as they neared her pickup truck. "Thanks for all the help."

"No problem. Maybe next time we can go for a ride or

something." Tori shook off most of the raindrops clinging to her curls.

Ashley lifted her hand to shake some of the rain from Tori's curls as well. "You're too cute for words, you know that?"

Tori mumbled a goodbye and ducked to hide her flushed cheeks. Ashley got in her truck and drove off. Tori watched her leave, trying to make sense of the different facades Ashley presented to the outside world. Which one was the true Ashley?

TORI WAITED UNTIL after her last class of the day to make her visit to the campus health office. She'd only been to the tiny facility once before, to get an ice pack for Matt when he'd walked into a tree. A cramped desk with no one behind it filled up the right hand side of the lobby, and a bench surrounded by racks of pamphlets and free samples of condoms and lube took up the left side. Tori scanned the pamphlets. What she was looking for was right below STDs and staying out of debt—a Planned Parenthood pamphlet. She tugged out the last copy and flipped through it.

"Can I help you, sir?"

She jumped at the voice behind her, folded the pamphlet, and stuffed it in her back pocket, ignoring the fact that she'd been called sir. "Um, no. I'm fine." She avoided eye contact with the middle-aged lady who now sat at the desk and rushed out the door.

She bumped into Jackie as she hurried away from the facility.

"Where are you off to?" Jackie stepped out of Tori's way as if she were a speeding car.

"No place." She glanced back at the health office. Not that she expected the lady to follow her out and demand to know if she were pregnant. This wasn't high school. They didn't care who was doing what, with or without protection.

"Hello? You still with us there, Tori?" Jackie waved a petite hand in front of her face.

"Very funny. What are you doing still on campus?"

Jackie crossed her arms. "Nothing much I suppose. Matt was supposed to meet me outside the Flint Center about an hour ago."

"He's late again?"

"Tell me about it." Jackie turned away from her. "So much for staying together through college."

"Don't say that." She draped an arm over Jackie's shoulder. "You know Matt. He's probably addicted to a new video game or something." The tension in Jackie's shoulders lessened as they started to walk. "Do you need a ride home? I'm done for the day."

"No, thanks. I've got my mom's car today."

"Let's go get a Jamba juice, then." She stopped when she heard a distant voice calling her name. She scanned the campus buildings around them but didn't see anyone she recognized. She was about to chalk it up to auditory hallucinations when Jackie pulled away from her.

"There he is." Jackie pointed to Matt as he appeared around the side of the health office. His dusty black boots pounded the pavement as he trotted up.

"Are you guys deaf?" he asked, panting. "I've been shouting your names since I got out of the parking lot."

Oblivious to Jackie's sour mood, he leaned down and kissed the top of her head.

Jackie scooted away from him when he tried to wrap an arm around her. Tori thought it was time she left the two of them alone to talk out their problems, but Matt chatted on, ignoring Jackie's subtle anger cues.

"How's it going, Tori? Anything new with that horse lady?" he asked with a mischievous look in his brown eyes.

She pulled her shirt down over the pamphlet, tucked in her back pocket, and remembered nobody knew about Ashley so he must be talking about Michelle. "She's just a friend. I'm getting some great experience helping her train the younger horses, though. And got paid for leading a couple of trail rides too."

"Not a bad deal," Matt said.

"I'm heading home," Jackie announced. "I'll see you tomorrow, Tori."

Matt's eyes widened as he watched Jackie stomp off. "What's that all about?"

Tori smacked him on the shoulder. "You blew her off, dude. Like an hour ago? You need to go apologize."

Matt took off after Jackie, rubbing his shoulder where Tori had hit him. Maybe she'd used a bit too much muscle behind it, but the guy needed to get his act together. She hoisted her backpack higher up on her shoulder and headed home.

A half hour later, she pulled up into the driveway and parked behind her mother's silver SUV. Why was her mother home so early? Their daily truce depended on the two of them spending minimal time in each other's company. Tori looped her backpack over her shoulder as she trouped up the immaculate, flower-lined walkway. Taking a chance that her mother would be in the main front room, Tori entered through the kitchen. Her mother was there on her cell phone, eyeing up Tori with her perpetual frown.

She locked the door behind her, avoiding eye contact with her mother. She'd grab a soda and get up to her room while her mother was on the phone. That should prevent any major flare-ups. She felt her mother's steady gaze as she opened the fridge and pulled out a Coke.

"You could at least drink diet Coke instead of a full-calorie Coke."

So much for the phone call. Tori deliberately grabbed a cookie and stuffed it in her mouth. She wouldn't succumb to her mother's fixation with weight control.

"Something's falling out of your pocket," her mother said as she pushed past her.

Tori whipped her hand back to grab the forgotten pamphlet, but it slipped through her fingers. Her mother stepped in and snatched it from the hardwood floor. Tori tried to grab it back, but it was already too late.

"What's this all about?" Her mother waved the pamphlet in front of her as if she wasn't aware of what had been in her own back pocket a minute ago.

"It's a Planned Parenthood information booklet. See, it has their name on the bottom, in friendly blue letters."

Her mother's expression darkened as her eyes skimmed the bold-faced words on the front page. Tori bit back a snide remark about privacy. She didn't have the heart to fight with her mother, she just wanted the information back to give to Ashley.

"Are you pregnant?"

Tori barked out a laugh. "Oh, yeah. Definitely. Triplets, I hope." She rubbed her stomach like the glowing moms-to-be did on TV.

"Back in the kitchen, now!"

"Look, it's a joke—"

"Now, Tori Kahl." The prominent vein across her mother's forehead throbbed.

Straight to silver medal, and she wasn't even trying. If she wasn't so ticked off about her mother's obvious assumption, she would have laughed out loud. As it was, she stomped back into the kitchen and hoisted herself up on the counter. She glared back at her mother in silence.

"This is not a condition to joke about."

Tori crossed her arms. "And what condition is that?"

A jumble of emotions distorted her mother's face in the span of a few seconds. "This condition." Her mother shook the pamphlet again.

Tori bent over, pretending to examine the paper in detail. "It's not so much a condition as a plan. Thus Planned Parenthood."

Her mother slammed the pamphlet on the table. "Don't be a wise-ass. If it's not you, then who is it? Robyn?"

Tori stared at the floor. "You don't know shit about Robyn."

"Watch your mouth, girl. It doesn't take a genius to realize she hasn't been around in months. If it's her, you should keep out of this. She won't thank you for convincing her one way or another on this decision." She waved the pamphlet again.

Whatever response Tori was considering, she discarded when Jerome came bounding through the kitchen door. He hated when they fought.

She hopped off the counter and held out her hand. "Just give me the pamphlet back."

"Not until you explain yourself." Her mother seemed oblivious to Jerome's discomfort. She hadn't even turned to acknowledge his presence.

Tori stuffed her fists into her pockets to keep from pounding them against the wall. "Fine, keep it." Giving it to Ashley wasn't worth the aggravation of putting up with her mother for another minute. She stormed out of the kitchen.

Her mother followed. "Just tell me you're not the one pregnant."

Tori whirled around so fast that she saw a glimmer of shock in her mother's eyes. "No, I'm not pregnant. Are you satisfied?"

"Are you sure?"

"Pregnancy's not really a risk for me, Mom. You better look to Jerome if you want to be a grandmother some day." A look of confusion crossed her brother's face as he watched them from the kitchen. Throwing up her hands in defeat, she stomped up stairs and slammed her bedroom door. She tossed her backpack against the closed door, hearing a thud as it landed on the carpet.

Her mother thought she could be pregnant. *Gee, Mom, I'm not, but I am a dyke. Is that better or worse in your eyes?* Her throat was dry. She rummaged through her backpack. She had a bottle from Jackie in there somewhere and now was a damn good time for it.

Chapter 5

THE LAST TENDRILS of a late morning fog drifted through the round pen as Tori worked in tandem with Michelle riding Ruby. Tori walked Buddy in a wide circle, regretting the grey sweatshirt that she'd forgotten to peel off before the lesson started. The mid-November morning coolness disintegrated with the fog, leaving her with a sheen of sweat under her warm clothes.

Buddy's ears flattened, and he side-stepped into Tori's space as Ruby and Michelle passed.

"Did you see that?" Michelle asked. "He's invading your space to keep away from Ruby. Don't let him do that."

Tori gave Buddy's lead rope a couple of flicks toward his neck, until he backed away from her. They resumed their walk for two more circles around the pen. Buddy remained attentive to her guidance.

"That's better. Now take him into the center and keep him listening to you. Ruby and I will try to distract him." Michelle directed Ruby into a fast walk around the outside edge of the pen while Tori kept Buddy standing in the center.

Whenever Buddy's focus moved to Ruby, Buddy flicked his lead rope to bring his attention back to her. Michelle urged Ruby into a slow trot. Buddy moved his hind end away from them, but otherwise remained focused. When Ruby broke into a canter, Buddy pulled back against the lead rope as if he wanted to join in on the fun.

"Control him," Michelle said as she cantered past a second time.

Tori walked toward Buddy's mid section until he yielded his back end away from her instead of Ruby. She was once again the focus of Buddy's attention and kept his focus on her by changing her position each time Ruby cantered by.

"Excellent." Michelle slowed into an easy walk. "I think he's done well for a two year old, don't you?"

Tori went to Buddy and rubbed his neck. "Yep, he's a good boy."

"We should call it quits for today." Michelle hopped off Ruby's back. "Always end a lesson on a good note for the horse." She unbelted the girth to Ruby's English saddle and pulled the saddle and blanket off.

Tori unclipped the lead rope from Buddy's halter and let him loose. He turned away from her and galloped off around the pen, kicking his back legs up a couple of times along the way. Tori waited for Michelle to unbuckle Ruby's bridle and hand it to her, then the two of them left the horses to play and roll in the sand pen while they took the tack back to Michelle's tack room.

Tori saw Ashley mucking out Tank Girl's stall. Ashley wore her long brown hair pulled back in a ponytail under a dusty 49ers baseball cap. The sleeves of her baggy blue sweatshirt were pulled up while she raked up manure and dumped it into a rusty wheelbarrow. Tori peeled off her sweatshirt and left it draped over the fence to Saxon's stall. He poked his big head over the fence and knocked her sweatshirt to the ground.

"Hey, watch the merchandise." She moved her sweatshirt out of his reach, then scratched under Saxon's chin. He stretched out to receive more attention.

With no sign of Ashley's grandfather around, Tori decided it was time to give her the Planned Parenthood pamphlet. She'd eventually gotten it back from her father after he had a more sedate discussion with her about it. Why couldn't her mother have taken the sane, understanding approach that he had? She wondered if her mother was going through menopause, or if she was just a bitch to the core.

She pulled the pamphlet out of her pocket. Her dirty fingers left marks on the edges, and she wiped her hands and the paper on her jeans to clean them off. When she turned around,

Ashley had finished mucking out Tank Girl's stall and was headed toward the muck bin with a very full wheelbarrow.

Tori trotted up next to her. "Hey."

Ashley gave her a crooked smile. "You're too damn energetic this morning."

She shrugged. "Just glad to be here and not at home." She followed Ashley to the muck bin and waited while she emptied the wheelbarrow. When Ashley rejoined her, she stopped procrastinating and handed over the pamphlet. "I picked it up at school."

When Ashley's smile faded away, she wanted to kick herself for being such an idiot. Of course Ashley wouldn't want her butting in. And what kind of help could she be anyway?

"Thanks," Ashley mumbled, looking around furtively. At least Tori had chosen a quiet area of the stables to make a fool of them both. They had twenty yards of scrub oak between them and the nearest stable.

"Sorry. I didn't mean to embarrass you or anything."

Ashley squeezed her arm. "No really, thanks." Her hand felt warm against Tori's bare arm. "I haven't figured out what to do about it, yet."

"Well, maybe that will help." She thought Ashley would just pocket the pamphlet, but instead she started reading it. Tori stuffed her hands in her pockets. Should she leave Ashley to analyze her options by herself? She was about to do just that when Ashley refolded the pamphlet.

"What would you do?" Ashley's brown eyes searched hers.

She's asking my advice? Tori shifted from foot to foot, unsure how to respond. She grasped at the first idea that came to mind. "You should go talk to them, the Planned Parenthood folks. They're supposed to be neutral. They won't try to convince you of one option or the other."

"You think so?" The pamphlet shook in her hands.

Tori thought she might start crying again, and she looked around to be sure no one else was heading their way. "Can't hurt to talk to them." Ashley's gaze locked on her again, her eyes glistening in the filtered sunlight. *I hate it when girls cry.* Tori resisted the urge to bolt.

Ashley's fist tightened around the pamphlet, creasing the edges. "I can't do this." She tried to hand it back to Tori.

"Keep it. I already got in enough trouble for it."

"Trouble?"

"My mother found it and gave me the ten-cent lecture about getting pregnant." She hadn't thought it was funny at the time, but Ashley had an infectious laugh that drew her in. "I think she'd have taken me for an abortion that minute if I really was pregnant."

Ashley's laugh ended as fast as it started.

Tori apologized. "I guess it's not a debatable issue for her."

"I wish it was as easy for me." Ashley leaned against the muck bin, staring at the Planned Parenthood pamphlet again.

"I'm the last person to give advice, but you've only got two options, and one of them has a clock going tick tickety tick against it."

Ashley frowned, staring into the distance. "Three options."

"Three?"

"Never mind." Ashley pushed off the muck bin, studying Tori for a moment. "Will you come with me?"

The softly spoken request took a moment to make sense to Tori's rattled brain. Before she could answer, Ashley looked away, stuffing the pamphlet in her pocket and grasping the wheelbarrow handles again.

"Sorry." Ashley shoved the empty wheelbarrow in front of her and started walking. "I shouldn't have asked."

Tori snapped out of her shock, went after her, and put a hand on Ashley's arm to slow her down. "No, no, it's just . . . You took me by surprise is all." She sucked in a breath, as if preparing for a deep dive. "I'll go with you, if you want."

Ashley slowed but didn't stop. "It's okay. You don't have to or anything."

"No, I want to. You shouldn't have to face this alone." She dipped her head down until her face was within Ashley's lowered gaze and grinned as a slow, crooked smile pulled at the corners of Ashley's lips.

They resumed their walk back to Tank Girl's stable.

"When did you want to go?" Tori asked.

Ashley stumbled over a stone in their path, tipping the wheelbarrow on its side. "Um, I don't know. Do you know where the nearest office is?"

She pointed to Ashley's pocket. "They're listed on the back."

Ashley glanced around before she pulled the pamphlet out and flipped it to the back side. Tori peered over her shoulder, scanning the list of sites stamped on the back. "The Alameda one is close."

"Too close." Ashley glanced up. "I'd rather go further away from here."

Tori studied the list again. "Santa Cruz? It says they are open every day but Sunday."

Ashley stared at the pamphlet until they heard the unmistakable clip-clop of a horse and rider. She rammed the pamphlet back into her pocket and started pushing the wheelbarrow again. Tori wandered over to Saxon while Ashley dumped the wheelbarrow outside Michelle's tack room. With a number of other horse owners wandering around, she didn't think Ashley would talk about her pregnancy anymore. She was surprised when Ashley grabbed her by the arm and dragged her into the relative privacy of Saxon's stable.

"Do you think you can go today?" Ashley asked. "To Santa Cruz?"

She spent most Saturdays helping Michelle around the barn, but Ashley's sudden resolve might not survive if she put off the visit. "Um, sure. When did you want to go?"

Ashley kicked at the bed of clean shavings, not looking at Tori as she spoke. "I was thinking maybe now?"

"Now," Tori repeated, feeling trapped in a whirlwind of her own creation. She looked at Ashley, and it finally clicked why this all made sense. Ashley needed someone outside her normal social circle, and Tori fit that description. She nodded in agreement.

"I'll drive. My car's over here." She pointed to her muddy blue Focus. She opened the passenger door and tossed things into the back seat. "Sorry about the mess. It's usually just my brother sitting here." After she cleared a spot for Ashley, she got in the driver's side.

The gas gauge said she had over half a tank, enough to get there and back. She flicked on the radio, and they drove without talking for most of the forty minute ride over the hill into Santa Cruz. A thick blanket of fog hung over the seaside town.

"Where's the office?" she asked.

Ashley leaned to the side and pulled out the pamphlet. "Pacific Avenue." She looked up at Tori. "I don't know that street."

"Do you want to give them a call and ask for directions from Route 1?"

Ashley pulled out her cell phone and dialed. Her voice sounded shaky as she talked. They had no pen between them, so she repeated the directions out loud for Tori.

All the beach tourists left Santa Cruz alone in cool weather so Tori had no problem finding a parking spot across from the office. She saw no sign of anti-abortion protesters and breathed a sigh of relief. Ashley didn't need some rabid fanatic slinging guilt at her for a decision she hadn't even made yet.

She waited for Ashley to lead the way. Ashley stared at the Planned Parenthood sign, then stepped out of the car. Tori followed her across the street and through the front door. Two women sat in the waiting room, one young and staring at the television, the other older and looking grim. Tori looked away when the one she assumed was the mother turned a dour gaze in her direction.

The receptionist was a woman in that unguessable age range that was older than Tori but younger than her mother. Ashley wandered to the information rack near the waiting room and thumbed through a couple of random pamphlets. Tori doubted she read any of them.

"Are you okay?" she asked in a whisper.

Ashley stepped back from the information rack. "Yes. Just nervous."

"We could go for a walk around the block first, if you want."

Ashley's jaw tightened, and she took in a deep breath. "No. Let's do this before I chicken out."

"You're only getting advice. You don't have to make any decisions today."

The tension in Ashley's jaw seemed to lessen. She flashed a weak smile at Tori and walked to the front counter.

The receptionist looked up at her. "Can I help you today?"

"I'm pregnant."

Tori cringed as a flush rolled up Ashley's neck and cheeks. She took a step closer, hoping her presence might lend some support.

The receptionist glanced at her, then returned her attention to Ashley. "If you'll sign in, we can have a counselor discuss your situation with you."

Ashley picked up the pen on the counter, but her hand hesitated over the sign-in sheet.

"Everything here is strictly confidential," the receptionist said. "No records of visitors ever leave here."

Ashley nodded once, then scribbled her name on the next open line. She put the pen back on the counter, walked to the waiting area, and sat as far from the other two occupants as she could. Tori sank into the chair beside her and looked around. It was like any other clinic, with the medical advice pamphlets stuffed in a magazine rack along with aged copies of *Women's World*, *Time*, and oddly, *Highlights* magazine for kids. Did women who already had kids come for abortions? Hell, they did offer more than just an avenue for abortions, something the regular protesters failed to recognize.

Sitting in the waiting room didn't seem like a good thing

for Ashley's nerves, so Tori rattled her brain for some topic of conversation. "What do you like to do, besides riding?"

Ashley glanced at her with a sly smile. "Sex."

Tori suppressed a groan. "Besides sex."

Ashley looked puzzled. "Not much. Reading, I guess."

"What do you read?"

"Romance books, mostly, or historical fiction. How about you?"

Romance? Tori couldn't imagine what a player like Ashley found in romance novels. "I like science fiction."

"Figures. That inner geek shines through. So what do you do? Besides ride and muck out a dozen stalls."

"Only seven stalls and that goes toward boarding Saxon. I'm looking for another job, though."

"Any luck?"

Tori sank further in her chair. "Not yet. I saw a Domino's ad for a night driver, but the manager won't be in until Tuesday night."

"Good luck with that."

Silence crept up between them. Ashley, picking at the rough skin around her fingernails, stared at the floor tiles. An orderly came out through a pair of glass paneled double doors to call in the young woman and her mother.

Tori could only see part of an antiseptic white corridor beyond the doors. Luckily, she wouldn't have to see anything beyond the waiting room. "I don't like hospitals."

Ashley seemed startled by the start of another conversation, but she stopped digging at her fingers and shifted in her chair to face Tori. "How come?"

Tori shrugged. "I've been in and out of them a lot."

"Were you sick?"

"No. Just clumsy."

Ashley laughed. "Did you fall off a lot of horses as a kid?"

"I wish it was just as a kid," she said. "My body just moves faster than my brain sometimes."

"When was the last time you were in the hospital?"

She leaned forward and pointed to the side of her head. "Stitches and a concussion. About nine months ago." She remembered being in a similar waiting room with Robyn holding her hand and growling at the emergency room nurse about something. "I ran into an air conditioning unit."

Ashley coughed in a lame attempt to hide her instinct to laugh. It was comical, after the fact.

"How about you? Have you been to the hospital a lot or not at all?"

Ashley's cheeks turned pink. "Just for, you know, the annual gyn."

"Oh." Tori hated those exams. Her mother forced her to go from the age of sixteen, and she had to explain to the doctor each time that yes, she was sexually active, but no, she didn't need birth control. That got her a blank stare until the doctor clued in that she was queer.

The double doors swung open again. This time, an older woman emerged, carrying a yellow folder. She called Ashley's name and smiled when Ashley stood up. "Your friend can come in with you, if you like," she said, looking between Ashley and Tori.

Ashley glanced back at Tori. "I'll go in alone, thanks."

Tori tried not to sound too relieved. "That's cool. I'll be outside when you're done." She watched Ashley walk into the long white corridor beyond the doors before she all but ran out the front door.

Cold air slapped her as she emerged from the facility. She inhaled, replacing the sterile clinic air with the scent of the ocean that blew around her. The fog had rolled back to reveal a blue sky spotted by white clouds. She had about fifteen minutes or more before Ashley finished. With no plan in mind, she ambled toward a multicolored flag fluttering in front of a store on the next block. It was a feminist bookstore.

Twenty-five minutes later, she headed back to the clinic. Her stomach did a somersault as she approached a small but obvious cluster of protesters. Two men dressed in creased white shirts and ties, and an older woman in a flowered skirt stood on the opposite side of the street from the Planned Parenthood office, holding up signs. They were far enough from the facility not to be an immediate threat, but close enough to harass anyone coming or going.

Tori slowed down, praying that Ashley hadn't tried to leave the office by herself. As she neared the front doors, she heard the older woman calling out to her. "Don't murder your unborn child!"

"You mean a gaggle of cells smaller than the head of a pin?" She didn't wait for an answer. She swung open the clinic door and ran into Ashley coming out. "Sorry, have you been waiting?"

Ashley was preoccupied with the paperwork in her hand, so Tori didn't press her further. They walked across the street, two car lengths from where the protesters stood glaring at her, but Ashley seemed not to notice. She opened the passenger door, and Ashley mechanically got inside. She gave a cheery wave to the protesters before she ducked into the car and drove off.

Tori made it back to the main street and headed toward the highway. "Are you hungry? We could find a sandwich shop before we drive back over the hill if you want."

Ashley shook her head. "Can we just go back home?"

"Sure." Her stomach growled in protest, but she headed back to the valley. Towering redwoods and pine trees edged the highway. Ashley stared at the passing blur of trees. Tori didn't ask what she'd talked about in the clinic. That was Ashley's private business. Instead, she turned on the radio for some background noise and drove over the summit and down into Santa Clara Valley.

As she passed a familiar ridge, she nudged Ashley. "That's where I live." She waved at the landscape on the left.

Ashley bent low to look out Tori's window. "Up there? It must be gorgeous."

"Yep. Smells a lot better than the valley, too." Tori flicked on the blinkers to prepare for the exit that led to Shadow Oak Stables.

"My house is down there, below the brown haze." Ashley pointed to the right, into the South Bay area. "My grandfather loves it there, but I think it's too hot in the summer. I'm glad to be in the dorm this year."

The conversation drifted off as they left the highway and drove through the side streets. Tori turned onto the dirt stable road.

"They gave me a bunch of stuff." Ashley lifted the papers in her lap.

Tori glanced down, but she couldn't tell what the papers were about. "Do you think you have enough information now to make a decision?" She pulled into a free parking spot. Three trucks, including Ashley's, sat in a circle around the parking area.

Ashley didn't move to unbuckle herself, so Tori sat as well, waiting. "Do you want to see what they gave me?"

Tori took the offered papers and flipped through them. There was the expected balance of options, from abortion to adoption after delivery, to keeping the baby. "Looks thorough. What do you think?" She handed the papers back to Ashley.

Ashley's brown eyes searched hers. "I," she began, and then swallowed, turning away from Tori. "I don't think I can go through with it."

Tori scrambled to guess which option Ashley was afraid of—delivering a baby or getting an abortion. "What part scares you?"

"All of it." Ashley tightened her fists around the paperwork. "It's too much like my mother." She turned back to Tori. "I don't even feel like I have a baby inside me."

Tori didn't understand the mother comment but hooked onto Ashley's last statement. "You're only a few weeks along. It's more like a clump of cells right now, isn't it?"

"A frigging complicated clump of cells that'll screw up my life no matter what I do."

Maybe Ashley had noticed the protestors. "I think what happened between you and your boyfriend was an accident, but that doesn't mean it has to ruin your life." She pulled out one of the papers that had caught her eye and read it quickly. "This says you could get a medical abortion. Not even an operation."

Ashley didn't answer, staring out the car window instead.

"I should just shut up though. This is something only you can decide."

"Yeah. Only I can decide." Ashley unbuckled and got out of the car. "Thanks." She stared at Tori through the window. "For everything. I owe you one."

Chapter 6

TORI WAS EXHAUSTED after a full day of classes and a nerve-wrecking job interview at Domino's Pizza. She pulled her car into the spot between her dad's truck and her mother's SUV. Lights were on in the kitchen, but she knew dinner was long since over. With luck, she could scrounge up some left-overs. Her stomach growled its frustration at her as she walked up the steps to the back door.

Her mother and father turned to Tori when she walked in and whatever conversation they were having ended. Having long since abandoned hope of understanding her parents, Tori mumbled her hello and headed for the fridge.

To her surprise, her father started the conversation. "Your mother and I need to talk to you."

"About?" Tori poked her head in the fridge. A tag-team parent discussion couldn't be a good thing, certainly not something she wanted to be a full participant in. She eyed up a container of leftover spaghetti and grabbed it.

Her mother lifted the container from her hands and popped it in the microwave. "Sit down, please, so we have at least some sense that you're listening."

Tori took a seat, glancing between her mother's frown and her father's tired expression. What had she done this time? She rattled her brain but couldn't come up with any offense worse than not taking her clothes out of the dryer the night before. A heinous crime, but not enough to warrant the two-headed lecture she was facing now.

Her father began, but as usual, her mother out-talked and out-gesticulated him until she was dominating the conversation. "It's time you realize you're living in an unrealistic bubble right now. High school and even college aren't the real world."

Thank God. High school was no dream and while college

lacked the direct teen aggression, it also lacked anything of interest to her. The beep of the microwave interrupted her mother's lecture, and Tori jumped up to grab a fork. She was starved.

Her mother sat across from her. "Maybe you aren't pregnant yet, but that doesn't mean you can keep playing with fire. You have to accept responsibility for your actions and your future."

Tori rammed a mouthful of hot spaghetti in her mouth to block the fit of giggles bubbling up inside her. Her mother was still on this track?

"I want you to go on the pill."

"Not really an issue, Mom." She finished the mouthful while she thought how to phrase it. If her father wasn't there, she'd have drawn out the fight just for fun. Instead, she decided on a glimmer of truth. "I'm not even seeing anyone right now, okay?"

Her father sighed. At least he sounded satisfied, which was more than she could say for her mother.

Her mother leaned forward. "You have four, maybe five years to get your life and your career on track. You mess up now and you'll be on the road to nowhere."

Now this was a familiar lecture. Tori munched on her leftovers while her mother droned on about college and careers. When she brought up employment, Tori couldn't stop herself from bragging. "I actually have a job. I start in two days."

"Great! I always knew you'd knuckle down." Her father pushed back his chair, signaling that he thought the lecture was over. She watched his retreating back, wondering if she'd be as lucky with her mother.

Her admission had knocked some of the wind out of her mother's sails, but not enough to stop her completely. "What kind of job?"

"Pizza deliveries, four nights a week."

Her mother didn't look pleased. "I was hoping you'd set your sights a bit higher."

"It's a job." She finished her dinner and rinsed off the container in the sink.

"You know you have a double mark against you already, Tori. You're black and you're female."

"I'm biracial. You don't get to toss away Dad's half of my DNA."

Her mother let out a harsh laugh. "Yeah, because that half is going to get you somewhere. I'm not looking for an argument. Just listen for once. Whether you like it or not, the outside world sees you as black, and they're going to assume you're not as capable or driven as someone else."

"Yes, Mother." Anything to end this nowhere conversation.

Her mother caught her before she could leave the kitchen. "Did you give that Planned Parenthood pamphlet to your friend?"

"Yeah." Tori narrowed her eyes. Where was this track going?

Her mother glanced around and then spoke in a low, icy voice. "You never knew your grandmother, so you don't know what this kind of situation did to her. She got pregnant back in the fifties and got herself a closet abortion. You know what she told me and your aunt Mattie before she died? She said she was going straight to hell for murdering that unborn baby."

For once, Tori was caught off guard and scrambled for something to say. "It's not the same now. Women get abortions all the time."

Her mother's smile wasn't reflected in her eyes. "Oh, it's legal now, but that's the only difference. There's still a world of guilt floating around out there just waiting to settle on the shoulders of some poor girl who thinks it's a no-brainer decision. A bag of guilt that'll last a lifetime." She stood up. "If you're sticking your nose in the middle of this, she better be a damned good friend."

Her mother left the kitchen. Tori sank back into a chair, relieved that the conversation was over. Between revelations about her grandmother and the cloud of doubt her mother dumped on her, Tori was glad she wasn't in Ashley's shoes.

TORI DROVE ASHLEY over the hill for what she hoped was the last time. She took the off ramp into downtown Santa Cruz and headed for the Planned Parenthood office. It was the Tuesday before Thanksgiving and traffic was lighter than normal, or at least lighter than it had been on her last visit. Ashley had gone through counseling, then a lab test, then a physical. She had only one thing left to do, and she'd told Tori she couldn't do it alone.

They sat in Tori's car with the engine idling in a parking spot a block away from the facility. Ashley wasn't moving. Would she change her mind? Tori couldn't picture herself in Ashley's situation. It was a world away from her reality.

Ashley stared at the Planned Parenthood building. "Abortion, adoption, or keep it. They don't tell you about the option my mother took."

"What did your mom do?" Tori hoped that option wasn't suicide. Ashley never spoke about her mother, and Tori assumed she was dead.

"She dumped me on my grandparents and never came back."

"Oh." What do you say to someone who was abandoned? Even with all the shit Tori gave her mother, she never had to worry about being deserted.

"I'd be nineteen when the baby's born."

She was keeping the baby now? Tori tried to keep up with Ashley's scattered thoughts. "Would you stay in the dorm?"

"I'd have to move back in with my grandfather in South San Jose and transfer to a community college to save money. He'd be pissed. Maybe. Mostly, he'd start looking at me the same way my uncles do, as the slut they always knew I'd turn into. Just like my mother."

Shit. That was one messed-up family. "Do you know your mom at all?"

Ashley rolled her shoulders and looked at Tori. "She lives up the peninsula. Last I heard, in South San Francisco. I'm not making the same decision she made, though."

Tori relaxed. "What's your decision?"

"Decision one—stop calling it a baby when it's only a gaggle of unwanted cells. Decision two—Get it over with."

Ashley got out of the car and headed for the clinic. Tori followed, glad to get decision two over with as well. Her mother was right. She was crazy to get involved in all this.

A woman stood outside the facility. Tori assumed she worked there until she stepped in front of Ashley and handed her a picture. Tori glanced over Ashley's shoulder at the blue-eyed baby smiling in the photo.

"Beautiful, isn't she?" The woman gave Ashley a motherly pat on the arm. "She's my granddaughter, and she'd be dead if her mother had come to a place like this."

Tori grabbed the picture from Ashley and shoved it back at the woman. "Fuck off."

Ashley's hands shook as she pushed open the clinic door, and they stepped inside. She leaned against the wall and shut her eyes.

Tori fought the urge to go out and kick the shit out of that woman. Just when Ashley seemed ready to accept her decision. Now, she could imagine the guilt piled up inside Ashley.

Tori glared at the receptionist. "Can't you do something about the asshole outside?"

The receptionist jumped from her chair and came out to them. "Damn, she's back." She took Ashley by the arm and led her to a seat in the waiting area. "I'm so sorry. I'll call the police and get her out of here."

Tori filled a paper cup from the water dispenser and handed it to Ashley. Ashley mechanically lifted the cup and drank. A man and a woman sat on the far chairs and gave her a sympathetic smile. Tori wondered if they had to pass through the same pious grandmother routine. From the pale look on the woman's face, she guessed yes, but the woman wasn't alone. She had someone to help her through it all. Tori wasn't great at the whole sympathy and support routine, but she'd make damned sure the nutcase outside didn't get a second chance at Ashley on the way out.

"Ashley Metcalf?"

Ashley looked up at the nurse, who was holding a door open for her. She looked back at Tori.

"Do you want me to stay here or come in with you?" Tori asked.

"Um. Maybe come in until they're ready to start?"

She got up and walked into the exam room with Ashley. She kept quiet during the long, slow process of getting Ashley checked, double-checked, questioned, and prepped, and then stepped out of the room while Ashley wrapped herself in a paper gown.

Ashley called her back in a minute later. The waiting was the worst. The last thing Tori wanted was to stand next to a scared shitless Ashley in a sterile examination room with nothing to do but stare at the cabinets or instruments they were about to use. Tori glanced at Ashley and looked away. It was awkward to see her look so vulnerable.

Ashley squirmed up onto the exam table. "I wish I hadn't put the decision off too long to take advantage of a medical abortion."

"It'll be okay." Platitudes. Was that the best she could come up with? "On the plus side, maybe we can find something interesting to steal in one of these cabinets?"

Tori opened the top cabinet. "More of these classy paper gowns. You want some more?"

The door opened. Tori jumped back and slammed the cabinet shut. Ashley wrapped her johnny tighter. The doctor came in, followed by the nurse who'd poked and prodded Ashley earlier. They gave Ashley the option of taking a mild sedative to relax her during the procedure, but she turned it down.

The doctor talked Ashley through the procedure, explaining each step. Tori wasn't listening anymore. She was thinking about her mother. If Tori were in Ashley's shoes, her mother would be standing right next to her, with a death grip on her arm, and a list of questions and demands to make of the doctors. Ashley had nobody.

69In Keisha's Shadow*

"Tori?"

Everyone stared at her. "Oh, sorry. Yeah. I'll be in the waiting room." She rushed out of the exam room and didn't stop until she was in the front lobby.

She looked outside, but the screwball grandmother was gone so she took a seat in the waiting room. She stared at the ceiling and counted tiles. When she finished, she counted holes in the tiles, but that proved to be impossible.

Ashley stepped into the waiting room, and Tori looked at the clock. Had it only been fifteen minutes? It all seemed surreal, like it was over too fast.

"Don't be an ass," she told herself.

"What?" Ashley's voice had that shaky edge that said maybe she'd been crying.

"Nothing. Just arguing with myself."

"And I thought I was screwed up."

Ashley settled the bill, and they left the clinic. It was over. Then again, the look on Ashley's face said maybe it was only just starting for her.

TANK GIRL TROTTED in a slow circle at the end of Ashley's lead line while Tori and Michelle rode their horses in a random pattern around the arena trying to distract Tank Girl. Tori thought Ashley had good control but she waited for Michelle to give the praise. She was grateful that Michelle had enough confidence in her ability to let her participate in the training sessions. She wasn't going to blow it by flapping her mouth instead of keeping quiet.

"Tank Girl's got great focus right now." Michelle hopped off her horse and handed the reins to Tori. "Can you take these two boys back to the stable? I think our girl here is ready for her first real riding lesson."

She hurried to take the horses back while Ashley tightened Tank Girl's saddle. By the time she returned, Michelle was draped over Tank Girl's back with one foot in the stirrup for balance.

"She looks steady," Tori said, entering the arena slowly so she didn't spook the horse. Michelle hopped off and onto Tank Girl's back a dozen times and only once did Tank Girl try to move away. Michelle grabbed the end of Tank Girl's rope halter and leaned over her back once again. This time, she pulled on the rope while tapping the horse's side. Tank Girl took a few steps in a circle in response to Michelle's commands.

Tori was amazed. It all looked too easy, but she knew Michelle had years of horse training experience behind her. She itched to have a turn at the one-stirrup walk with Tank Girl but she knew better than to ask. Michelle wouldn't let anyone else on the horse until well after New Year.

"Okay, I think she's had enough for one day." Michelle hopped off and handed the lead rope back to Ashley.

They all left the arena together, but she and Michelle took a few steps ahead when Ashley's cell phone rang. Tori watched Ashley out of the corner of her eye while they waited. She couldn't hear the words, but Ashley's voice was deeper than normal, and she let out a low chuckle.

"She's doing pretty good, all things considered."

She looked back at Michelle. "Ashley?" Did Michelle know what Ashley was going through? She thought Ashley wasn't talking about it, but maybe she just wasn't talking about it to her.

Michelle elbowed her. "Tank Girl. She's got good focus. She'll be a great show horse some day."

Ashley led Tank Girl forward again. "Sorry for the interruption. That was tonight's hot date."

Michelle laughed. "You never give it a rest, do you?"

"Too many datable people out there. Someone's got to show them a good time."

Michelle opened the gate to Tank Girl's stable. "Sounds like too much work to me."

"That's because you only date guys. You should experiment with a girl sometime." Ashley led her horse into the stable and removed her saddle.

Ashley's flirt switch wasn't just back in the on position, it was in overdrive. Tori thought it might be a reaction to the abortion, but Ashley had made it obvious to her that the whole topic was off-limits.

"How about you?" Michelle asked, nudging Tori. "Any hot dates tonight?"

She kicked the dirt with her boots. "Nope."

Ashley popped out of her stable and looped her arm through Tori's. "I'm available whenever you want to change that."

She sidestepped away from Ashley. "No thanks. Dating just leads to trouble and complications."

Ashley's smile faltered, and Tori realized Ashley had taken her words the wrong way. Before she could figure out a way to apologize, Ashley was leaving.

"Do you have time to help me feed?" Michelle asked.

She watched Ashley disappear down the trail to the parking lot. "Um, yeah. Give me a few minutes, okay?" She didn't wait for an answer. She ran and caught up with Ashley at her truck. "Hey."

Ashley turned to her. Her former smiling face was clouded over but Tori couldn't tell if it was anger, embarrassment, or something else.

Tori made sure no one was within hearing distance. "I didn't mean anything by what I said, you know."

Ashley gave her a silent nod.

"I was talking about the problems I had with my ex-girlfriend."

A glimmer of Ashley's former smile returned. "I knew it. You *are* gay."

Tori gave a half smile. "As gay as you are bi." When Ashley's smile disappeared again, Tori struggled for what to say next. She didn't want to bring up the pregnancy if Ashley didn't. "Is everything okay?"

Ashley's expression hardened. "Fine."

With nothing else to say, she took a step back. "Well, see you next time."

"What are you up to?"

She didn't know if Ashley was prolonging the conversation or just being polite. "I'm helping Michelle feed and then I have to prepare to fail my next history test."

Ashley laughed. "Do you have a specific study sheet that helps you fail or do you play it by ear?"

"No. It's a God-given talent when it comes to this subject."

Silence surrounded them again, and Tori figured she ought to leave.

"Come to my place tonight."

Was Ashley coming on to her again? No, there was nothing flirtatious in her expression.

"I'm a history major, remember? I can help you pull off a nice steady C instead of failing maybe?"

"I thought you had a date?"

Ashley shrugged. "I can change that to another day. Come on, I owe you one."

She saw a hint of sadness in Ashley's eyes but didn't question it. "You're sure you're up to this? I'm seriously dense when it comes to memorizing dates and shit."

Ashley's smile returned in full. "I think I can handle it."

TORI HELD THE cell phone in one hand and drove with the other, hoping her battery lasted until she made it to Ashley's place. "Okay, I'm on the Alameda now."

"Great," Ashley said. "Do you see Santa Clara University coming up on the right?"

"Yeah."

"Take the second left after El Camino. Bellarmine Hall is hard to miss. You'll have to park on the street."

"Okay. See you in a few."

Tori stuffed her phone in her pocket. Two minutes later, she took the second left and parked a block away from Ashley's dorm. She entered the three-story building behind a group of teenage boys who were whispering about sneaking into a keg party.

The night guard didn't say a word until Tori passed by his desk. "I need to see your resident ID."

Tori watched the boys disappear down the hall and wondered why she was the only one worth stopping. "I don't live here. I'm visiting a friend."

The guard pushed a phone in her direction. "Your friend has to come down and clear you before I can let you in."

Tori ignored his phone and called Ashley back on her cell phone. "Hey, It's Tori."

"Did you get lost?"

"Um, no. I'm down in the lobby. There's a security guy here who says you have to come let me in."

"I wonder who he's trying to impress by being a pain in the ass. I'll be right down."

Tori slouched against the near wall and glared at the paunch-bellied guard who sat at the desk reading a magazine. Ashley appeared in the stairwell, dressed in an oversized university sweatshirt and sweatpants. Tori glanced at her torn jeans and decided she'd dressed appropriately.

Ashley waved at the guard. "She's with me."

He gave them both barely a glance before returning to his reading. Tori followed Ashley up two stories to her room. A desk and two beanbag chairs separated the two beds. Tori didn't think to ask if Ashley had a roommate. She took in the decorations tacked to the wall above each bed and guessed the one with the Hooters tank top was Ashley's.

Ashley sat down under the tank top and patted the bed next to her. "Have a seat."

Tori stood in the middle of the tiny room, her backpack hanging from one hand. "You don't have to do this, you know."

With an exaggerated sigh, Ashley took Tori's backpack and set it on the bed. "Are you always this resistant to a bit of help?"

"You have no idea."

Ashley's crooked smile convinced Tori this wouldn't be a flirt-fest. She settled on the bed and pulled out her book and notes.

She gave Ashley a handout that listed the topics on the final. "We don't have to go over all of it."

Ashley rolled her eyes. "Let's see your class notes."

She handed over her notebook.

Ashley flipped through the pages. "Interesting doodles. What's this one?"

"That would be my mother. See how the vomit burns through the kitchen table but leaves her briefcase intact?"

Ashley leaned closer, her shoulder brushing against Tori's. "Coconut perfume?"

"Huh? Oh, no." Tori blushed and shifted away. "It's hair oil, the only thing that keeps it from being an even frizzier mess."

"It looks good. Your hair, I mean." Ashley lifted a hand as if to touch Tori's hair but then jerked it back. "So, um, where do you want to start?"

Tori shrugged. "Anywhere. It's not like I remember any of it."

For the next hour and a half, Ashley outlined the relevant points in Tori's history book and then quizzed her on critical issues. Tori's eyes started to droop half-shut and she was about to call it a night when she heard someone rattling keys in the door. Her head shot up in time to see a Latina woman enter. She carried a leather bag and wore a dress that wrapped around her perfect curves.

Ashley tapped her knee. "Hate to break the staring, but I think you're studied out for tonight."

The new woman dropped her bag and sank on the bed next to Tori. "I'm Carmen, by the way. And you are?"

"Tori." She shook Carmen's hand and thought she felt Carmen hesitate before letting go.

"So are you two, you know?" Carmen asked.

Ashley slammed Tori's book shut. "I was just helping Tori study."

Carmen's gaze wandered over Tori in an obvious attempt to test the waters. "How did you two meet?"

"We board our horses at the same stable," Ashley said.

Carmen was obviously gay, or maybe bi like Ashley. The two of them were perfect for each other. Tori got the uncomfortable feeling that maybe the two of them were a couple and three wouldn't be a crowd with the way Carmen was looking at her.

She hopped off the bed and piled up her notes and book. "Yeah, I guess we're done for the night."

Ashley stood up. "I hope it helped."

"It did, thanks." She slung her backpack over one shoulder. "Think fascist-guard will let me out of the building without a hall pass?"

Carmen kicked off her heels. "You must be talking about Franco."

"You know him?" Ashley asked.

"I had to show him my student ID, dorm card, and license before he'd let me in the first night."

"He takes his job seriously," Tori said.

Carmen let out a harsh laugh. "Only with people like us, chica." She nodded toward Ashley. "I bet you've never had a run-in with him."

"I never paid any attention."

"Humph. Some of us don't have that luxury." Carmen leaned back against the wall.

"You sound like my mother," Tori said.

"Then she's a smart woman."

Ashley looped her arm through Tori's. "If he bothers you again, I'll file a complaint." She winked as she led Tori to the door. "I know how to treat a girl."

Tori cringed at the lame line. Ashley was fumbling, and she didn't know why.

She extricated herself from Ashley's grasp. "Thanks, but I'll be fine." She knew she was darting away like a scared rabbit. It wasn't the impression she wanted to leave Ashley with, but the flirt competition between Ashley and Carmen was more than she bargained for.

Tori hurried out of the building, past a different guard

who never looked up from whatever she was reading. Back in her car, she blared music from her iPod, but the noise wasn't enough to distract her wandering thoughts. Ashley had been fun to be with for most of the night, until Carmen showed up. Then a different Ashley emerged—the one Tori was used to seeing in public. Ashley the flirt who saw everything through sex-tinted glasses. It wasn't the Ashley she liked, not the one that made her think "what if" now and then.

Not that the "what if" mattered. Even if she was up for dating, Ashley was too busy sleeping with anything that moved, including Carmen from the looks of it. She'd drive Tori crazy.

Sometimes, she did already.

Chapter 7

TORI SAT ACROSS from Jackie at Burger King. Matt was still in line at the register, but that didn't stop Jackie from digging into her food. Tori unwrapped her own but didn't start eating yet.

"You waiting for an invitation?" Jackie asked.

"Maybe I'm being polite and waiting for your boyfriend to get here."

Jackie pretended to choke on her food. "You? Polite?"

"It happens."

"Not often. Seems more like you're just not interested in food. And that, my friend, only happens when you're thinking about boinking someone." Jackie's eyes narrowed. "So who is it? Michelle?"

Tori laughed. "No, I'm not that pathetic. She's one hundred percent het, just like you."

Jackie bounced her thin eyebrows. "I'm not as heterosexual as you think, girlie."

"You're het enough, and so is Michelle."

"Okay, then who has you bypassing the foodstuffs then?"

A flush crept up Tori's cheeks. "Nobody." Her thoughts bee-lined to Ashley, but she'd never admit that. Jackie could be merciless with the teasing.

"You're such a bad liar."

"Shit. I said nobody, give it a rest." Whatever ridiculous thoughts Tori was having about Ashley weren't going anywhere. She hadn't even seen her for the past week.

"You're moody as all hell." Jackie took another bite of her hamburger and glared at Tori.

"It's been a shitty day." She had the nastygram her mother had tacked to her bedroom door for not getting her laundry out of the dryer. And then there were the two long essays she needed to finish by Friday but hadn't started.

Matt joined them at the table, holding his own bag of fast food poison. His dinner entailed two burgers, fries, and three apple pie desserts. Tori glanced at her own unappetizing choice of a chicken sandwich and milkshake. She pushed the sandwich away and took a long draw from her shake.

"You not hungry?" Matt asked.

"We were just discussing her lack of pleasantness." Jackie waved a thin finger at Tori. "So what's got you ticked off today?"

Tori picked the first thing that popped into her head. "I got that C on the history quiz we got back today."

Matt spoke over a mouthful of burger. "Better than the D you got last time."

She'd hoped to do better after Ashley's tutoring session. Maybe next semester she'd get more into the whole study thing. She groaned, thinking about what her mother's reaction would be.

"If your face drooped any more it'd be a puddle on the floor," Jackie said.

Tori leaned on the table with her elbow. "Just wondering how pissed off my mother's going to be when I fail this class."

Matt patted her shoulder. "Come on, you haven't failed, yet. You could pull it through on the final."

"Nice platitudes." Jackie rummaged in her bag. "This should help."

Matt covered Jackie's hand. "Do you have to do that here?" He glanced around the room.

Jackie pulled her hand free. "Relax, boy scout." She waved a little package in front of his face. "Not liquor this time. Just some brain stimulation herbs."

Matt glowered at Jackie as he bit his sandwich. One of these days, she'd push him too far. Tori didn't want to be around to witness it.

Too many bad thoughts clambered for attention in her head.

She took the package from Jackie. "Anyone up for a drink. I know where there's a keg party we could crash."

Jackie jumped at the idea, but Matt shrugged. "Sorry, I've got stuff to do."

"What stuff?" Jackie's voice took on a sharp edge, and Tori felt another fight coming on, this time her fault.

He grabbed up the rest of his food and stuffed it back in the bag. "Family stuff, for my uncle." He leaned over to kiss Jackie but she brushed him off. "I'll see you two tomorrow."

Jackie stared at him as he left. Tori couldn't stand the tension anymore and stood up. "Let's go before the keg's dry."

Jackie glanced at her and then back to the door Matt had just left through. "Yeah, I could use a drink."

Me, too, Tori thought.

TORI HEADED BACK home at three in the morning. A light drizzle spattered her windshield as she took the highway exit that led to the mountain road where she lived. She had the road to herself at this hour and took advantage of the chance to accelerate through the curves, hearing her tires squeal on a particularly sharp turn.

The slow swish-swish of the windshield wipers mesmerized her. She could have turned them off, but the steady beat was the only sound in the car. Her iPod was buried in her backpack somewhere, and none of the radio stations came in clearly this far from the valley.

Her eyelids drooped. She slowed down when the road narrowed a mile away from her house. She wasn't drunk, though, just tired. That's what she told herself when her focus slipped from the road to watch the misty rain illuminated by her headlights. Her thoughts drifted to Jackie's worries about Matt. Jackie was sure he was cheating on her. That was the only explanation she had for why Matt had so many more "family stuff" issues. Jackie wouldn't come right out and accuse him of it. She wasn't that straightforward.

A familiar stone wall appeared in the narrow beam of Tori's headlights. She cut fast to the left, into her driveway. An instant later, she heard the sound of scraping metal and hit the brakes.

Cursing, she got out of the car and walked through the beam of her headlights to check the damage. Water from the over-hanging trees dripped heavy drops on her as she gazed into the darkness beside her car. There was no way she'd be able to see what happened without a flashlight. The road had given up on street lights five miles back.

She climbed back into the car and took the rest of the driveway at a crawl. She scanned each window of the house as she approached. No lights were on except the porch light and then the motion-sensitive security light that flicked on when she pulled in next to her father's truck. Happiness was a driveway long enough to hide the sound of an idiot moment at three in the morning.

Once in the house, she took the time to plaster a bagel with cream cheese before heading up to her room. With her eyes closed, she lay on top of the crumpled comforter on her bed and munched her snack. The room spun just a little bit, but not enough to worry about. Her bagel wouldn't be making a second visit.

Her mind drifted on the edge of sleep. A little voice inside her congratulated her on not getting into trouble. That faded into the bittersweet memory of a searing kiss. Lips locked, hands entwined in silky hair, the sensations felt so real. She knew where this memory ended, but her sleepy mind resisted the urge to block it.

Her last conscious thought was mild confusion about why her memory-vision involved long brown hair instead of Robyn's spiky blond hair.

"TORI KAHL, GET your butt out of bed right now."

Tori buried her head under the pillow but that shrill voice still broke through. Her head pounded in sync with her heartbeat and her mouth tasted like something had crawled into it and died overnight. Or maybe it had been dead before it crawled in. She didn't know. What she did know was the tone of her mother's voice meant she'd reached bronze medal status without even crawling out of bed. Forcing herself to a sitting position, she realized that accomplishment might be the highlight of her day.

"Tori!"

The fist pounding on her door did wonders for her headache, but not in a good way. "I'm up."

"Then get dressed and downstairs. You've got some explaining to do."

She examined her attire. No major stains, if you ignored the white smear just over her left shoulder. She brushed that off with an old sock, then crawled her way to the bathroom to work on a solution to her headache.

Four Advil and a quart of water later, she was sitting in the kitchen, cringing at every shrill syllable her mother shouted at her. It took three tries before she could follow the conversation. "What's wrong with my car?"

"Am I talking to a wall? I said it has a two foot gash on the side. What did you do?"

She went outside to take a look. Her mother followed at her heels. Tori walked three quarters of the way around her car when she saw the damage. "Shit."

"Shit is right. What did you do?"

Running a finger along the silver scrape that ran the length of her right front fender, she tried to remember what happened last night. She'd gone drinking. The pounding in her head told her that, even if she hadn't already remembered that part of her night. She also remembered being pretty damned sleepy on the way home. "Oh, now I remember. I took the driveway turn too wide."

"That's it? Just took it too wide?" Her mother crossed her arms and waited.

The throbbing pain in Tori's head quickened. "Guess I was tired."

"What the hell time did you get home last night?"

"I don't know. After midnight." Tori leaned against the side of her car to cover the dent she just noticed.

"Don't tell me you were out goofing off with your friends until that hour. We talked about this already. You may be an adult, but so long as you're under my roof, you'll keep my rules. And that includes coming home at a decent hour."

Tori crossed her arms, mimicking her mother. "So you want me to quit my night job? Because that's what kept me out that late."

Her mother raised one well-plucked eyebrow. "You were delivering pizza past midnight?"

"Until midnight. Then I went to McDonalds to eat. Then I peed. Then I came home." The lies came easy. Maybe she had a future in politics.

"Working late doesn't excuse reckless driving. You're responsible for this car. It's the only one we'll ever buy you."

Good. The little blue Focus wasn't her idea of a chick magnet. She wanted a truck. Of course, that meant actually working instead of lying about working.

Her mother stormed back into the house. Alone now, Tori examined the damaged fender. It wasn't too bad. Besides, it was the passenger side. She'd almost never see it anyway.

With the adrenaline from the fight dissipating, Tori's headache slowed back down to a persistent throb. In an hour, even that should disappear with the amount of Advil she'd swallowed. She glanced at the scrape one last time. No, she hadn't been too drunk to drive. It must have been just lack of sleep.

"STAYING STILL IS not going to stop me from kicking you in the ribs." Michelle sat in her saddle and emphasized her words with more taps on Tank Girl's sides, but the horse resisted her efforts to get her to walk forward.

Tori leaned over the round pen railing next to Ashley and stifled the urge to laugh. "She's as stubborn as her owner."

Ashley jabbed her in the ribs. "Not funny."

She held her side as if in agony, but she wasn't fooling anyone. She gave up the pantomime and returned to her spot by the railing. Michelle continued to pressure Tank Girl for some forward movement, and Tank Girl continued to resist. They stayed at a stalemate for fifteen minutes.

"Maybe it's too early for her."

Ashley glared at her over the rim of her sunglasses. "Are you talking about me or my horse?"

"If the shoe fits . . ." Tori's wisecrack earned her another jab, but she couldn't help herself. Ashley's bloodshot eyes and extra-large mug of coffee emphasized just how much she hated being awake at eight o'clock on a Saturday morning. She was an easy target for Tori's jibes.

Tori on the other hand, got paid to be at the barn by eight on the weekends to feed so Michelle had time for lessons. Ashley didn't have to show up for the lessons, but she did, every Saturday, and Tori admired her for that. Most horse owners just left it up to the trainer to break in their horse. They didn't get involved until the young horse could walk, trot, and canter. Ashley was different. Tori glanced at her while she was busy watching Tank Girl. Different in a good way.

"If I didn't know better, I'd think you were checking me out." Ashley's focus never left her horse, but she grinned as she sipped her coffee. "Haven't got anything better to do on a Saturday morning?"

Tori leaned over the railing to distract from the flush creeping up her cheeks. "Nope, nothing better to do."

Ashley turned to her. "So you admit you were checking me out?"

She just shrugged. For once, she had no snide comeback. What did it matter if Ashley caught her this one time. Didn't Ashley flirt incessantly with anyone and everyone anyway? It didn't mean anything.

Ashley's gaze whipped back to the round pen, and Tori looked just in time to see Tank Girl's first few steps. Ashley let out a whoop, spilling some of her coffee in the process, but she didn't seem to care.

Michelle stopped the pressure on Tank Girl's side, and the horse ambled to a stop a moment later. She patted Tank Girl's neck. "See? That wasn't so hard, was it?"

"Are you going to try again?" Tori asked.

"No. Always end a lesson on a good note, if you can." She slipped her feet out of the stirrups and lowered herself to the ground.

Ashley shoved her coffee mug at Tori and scrambled into the round pen. She buried her face in Tank Girl's unmanageable mane, but Tori saw the wide grin before it disappeared. Why couldn't Ashley be that down to earth the rest of the time?

Ashley led her horse back to its stable. Tori followed and waited until Ashley stored her tack before handing back her mug.

"That was worth getting up for," Ashley said before finishing off her coffee in one long gulp. She wiped her mouth on the sleeve of her denim shirt. "What are you up to now?"

"Me? Nothing until the evening feed."

"Let's go to the beach."

Tori stared at her, not sure how to take the invitation. They hadn't gone anywhere together since their ride to Planned Parenthood. They got on well enough at the stable, but she wasn't sure a full day with Ashley was a good idea, especially after being caught checking her out.

"Come on, we can take the horses and go for a ride." Ashley winked at her. "I promise I won't bite."

Without a truck and trailer, her rides were limited to the stable and the adjacent county open space preserve. A chance to ride on the beach was worth spending the day with Ashley.

Chapter 8

TORI DROVE TO the nearest sandwich shop while Ashley cleaned out the back of her truck to make room for their tack and hooked up her trailer. By the time she got back with sandwiches and soda, Ashley was leading Apostle to the trailer. She put the food on the front passenger seat and helped her load Saxon.

"Sorry," she said when they finally got him in. "He doesn't get out much."

Ashley lifted the trailer ramp and locked it in place. "We'll have to work on that."

Tori didn't know if that was an offer for trailer training, or a weak attempt at flirting, but she let it go. If she got paranoid about everything Ashley said for the next three or four hours, it would be a long day.

They rattled north, heading toward Half Moon Bay. The drive gave her plenty of opportunity to watch Ashley, and that didn't help her budding crush. Neither did the way Ashley kept her involved in the conversation, no matter what it was about. The flirt switch wasn't on, or if it was, she wasn't noticing. When they arrived at the beach, she hopped out of the truck to get some distance between them before she made a fool of herself.

Ashley grabbed the food Tori left behind and stuffed it in a backpack. Tori unlatched the loading ramp, and they backed Saxon out first, then Apostle, and tied them to the side of the trailer to tack up. Tori jammed a riding helmet on her head, but Ashley took the time to pull her brown hair back into a low ponytail before strapping on her own helmet.

"Do you need a leg up?" Tori asked.

"Yes, please."

She cupped her hands under Ashley's raised knee. She was

close enough to smell Ashley's perfume, the light aroma of vanilla wrapping around the scent of leather. Ashley grabbed her reins and on the count of three, hopped up while Tori lifted.

Apostle didn't move at all while Ashley slipped her feet into the stirrups. "Thank you kindly."

She glanced up to see Ashley's sly smile and knew she'd been played. "You didn't need a leg up, did you?"

Ashley shrugged. "How could I refuse a gallant offer from such an adorable dyke?"

She'd walked into that one and didn't bother replying. She hoisted herself into Saxon's saddle and took a moment to adjust her reins before she led the way down the path to the sandy beach.

The fog that hung to the coast dissipated as they trotted along the surf line. The salty breeze floated in from the pounding waves. Saxon loved it, kicking up spray with each prancing step. The beach was empty except for someone flying a kite in the distance.

"Want to race?" she said.

Ashley didn't bother to answer, but shot off down the beach at a gallop. Tori guided Saxon into a fast gallop on the hard, wet sand beyond the surf. By the time Ashley realized Tori was no longer in the waves, they were racing past her.

The effects of racing Ashley down the deserted beach left Tori sweaty and just a little bit aroused, much to her embarrassment. When they stopped to eat, she handed Ashley Saxon's reins and ran to the water's edge. The surf splashed up her work boots, but they were waterproof. Salt stains couldn't make them look any worse than the caked on mud anyway. She splashed water over her face until the cool sting erased her embarrassment. She jogged back to where Ashley was setting up a makeshift picnic. Both horses were tied to a large driftwood trunk, and Ashley sat further along the faded log, clutching two sodas.

She gave one to Tori. "You know, that rough and tumble dyke thing really works for you. I envy you that."

Tori cracked open her soda, letting some of the excess fizz drizzle into the sand. "Don't know what there is to envy."

"That's half the allure."

Tori covered her embarrassment by taking a long drink from her soda.

Ashley's crooked smile faded. "Go on a date with me."

Tori choked on her drink, sending a spray of soda drops across the sand. "What?"

Ashley grinned. "A date. You know, two girls, soft lighting, see where it goes from there?"

"I don't think I'm your type." Tori wiped her mouth on her shirtsleeve. This was turning into a freaky afternoon. Why had she agreed to join Ashley in the first place? Ashley was hot. Tori couldn't deny that. She got a kick out of knowing Ashley was interested in her, but did that mean she was willing to take things to the next level?

"So, what's my type, then, if not a rough, sexy dyke who can sometimes out-ride me?"

"Sometimes?"

"Don't push it." Ashley narrowed her eyes but she was still grinning. "So, a date?"

Tori sipped her soda, stalling while she struggled with an answer. She hadn't gone out with anyone since Robyn had dumped her. She enjoyed Ashley's company, and was crushing on her big time, so why was she hesitating?

Ashley let out a long sigh. "I didn't think it would be such a hard decision. I'm great on a date, if that wasn't obvious."

Her body language shifted to the exaggerated flirt that Tori had seen before, directed at multiple women. "Let's just stay friends, okay?"

Ashley leaned away from her, a deep frown on her face. *Some people don't take rejection well*, Tori thought. Happy she'd dodged that bullet, she opened the backpack and pulled out the sandwiches. "You want ham and cheese or Italian?"

She held up both. Ashley grabbed the Italian and unwrapped it in silence.

Tori unwrapped her ham and cheese and started eating. After a couple of bites, she noticed that Ashley wasn't eating. She hadn't dodged that dating bullet quite yet. "What's up?"

Ashley studied her for a long time, making Tori wish she'd just kept eating. "I know you like me. I saw you watching me on the drive over."

Tori shrugged. "So?"

"So why'd you say no to a date?"

She put her sandwich down on the wrapper. "Finding someone hot isn't a good enough reason to start a relationship."

Ashley laughed. "I wasn't asking for a relationship, just a night out."

"And that's why I said no." Tori picked up her sandwich and started eating to mask her frustration. She and Ashley were a world apart on how they looked at dating and sex. They'd never be a good match.

ASHLEY'S FLIRT-SWITCH was off, hopefully for good. The radio filled the silence on the ride back to the barn but Tori couldn't sit still for another half hour of mute Ashley. She picked what she hoped was a neutral topic.

"What's up with your grandfather? He hasn't been around the barn much lately."

Ashley gripped the steering wheel with white knuckles. "Damn it."

"What?"

"Nothing." Ashley kept her eyes on the highway. "Things aren't going well in that department."

She could only think of one thing that could go wrong between Ashley and her grandfather. "Did you tell him about the abortion?"

"What? No." Ashley's attention bounced between Tori and the highway. "You think that's the only thing going on in my life? Well, it's not. I did it and it's over, so just drop it, okay?"

"Fine." Tori stuck her boots on the dashboard and stared out the window. *Shit*. So much for the neutral topic. Mute Ashley was a step up from bitchy Ashley.

Tori's cell phone rang as the exit for the barn came up. She looked at the phone and recognized her mother's phone number. She accepted the call. Anything was better than Ashley's silent treatment.

"Yeah," she said.

"Answer the phone properly, please."

Tori rolled her eyes. "Hello, Mother. This is your daughter, how may I help you?"

"Why do I bother."

"Beats me." Tori watched the familiar streets roll by. Maybe she'd call Jackie after she finished at the barn. A beer or three were in order after today.

"You're brother needs a ride home. He's at Jacob's house."

So much for the beer plan. "Why can't you get him?"

"Because I asked you to."

"Fine, but I have to feed the horses first." Tori rammed the cell phone back into her pocket.

"Problems with your mother?" Ashley asked.

"She's a psycho bitch."

Ashley turned into the stable parking lot. "I know the feeling."

"Yeah, right."

Ashley hit the brakes too hard and the trailer hitch groaned in protest. "You think you're the only one with a messed-up mother? Try an alcoholic screw-up who left you behind and only remembers your birthday once every five years or so. You want to trade mine for yours?"

Shit. Another minefield topic. "Sorry I brought it up." She hopped out of the truck and slammed the door shut. What a miserable day this turned out to be.

They unloaded Saxon first, and then Ashley grabbed Tori's tack from the back of the truck. "You want this in your tack room?"

Tori hefted the saddle and pad from Ashley's arms and

tossed them over Saxon's back. "No thanks, I'm going for a ride."

"This close to feeding time?"

Tori grabbed the bridle. "Yes, this close to feeding time." She knew as much about horses as Ashley did. Saxon would be fine.

Ashley backed off. "Have fun." She turned back to the trailer to get Apostle out.

Tori paused. She shouldn't leave Ashley to take care of everything else, even if she was being a moody bitch. "Do you need help?"

"No, thanks."

It was a lot easier to get a horse out of a trailer than into one, so Ashley could handle it on her own. Given Ashley's bitchy mood, Tori would rather not have to help.

The air turned cold as evening approached. Tori took Saxon to the arena and cantered for a good twenty minutes, but it didn't help her frustration with Ashley or her mother.

She dismounted, stripped off Saxon's tack, and tossed a couple of flakes of hay at him before she went to feed the rest of the horses.

Ashley was grooming Apostle in his stable when Tori dropped off Apostle's two flakes of hay. Ashley didn't say a word to her. Big surprise.

Tori finished the rest of her feeding rounds and moved Saxon back to his stable. She tossed another couple of flakes at him. As she drove away, she saw just enough in the growing dark to realize Ashley's truck was the only one left in the parking lot.

TORI STRADDLED THE fence to the closed hiking trail, staring at the shadows within shadows that formed the tree line. She shouldn't be in the trail head parking lot after dusk, but she'd already dumped Jerome at home, late in her mother's eyes of course. No one cared where she was now. She shivered as the night air bypassed crisp and hovered around damned cold. There would be frost by morning. Her mother's miniature rose bushes would take a beating since Tori had forgotten to wrap them against the cold.

Just another thing for her mother to be pissed off at her about, another item for the list of Tori screw-ups for the week. She pulled out her pocket knife and toyed with the tip of it. She had to get the hell away from that house. The pizza job and mucking out weren't enough to buy her way to freedom in an apartment somewhere. That meant four more years of hell until she graduated college. Maybe then she'd be good enough in her mother's eyes.

She barked out a harsh laugh as she rolled up her shirt sleeve. It would be longer than four years. She'd never pass all her classes and that made her a failure. She'd never match up to Keisha, perfect Keisha, with the good grades and perfect attitude. Just like her mother.

The first cut she made into her forearm stung, leaving a thin red line. The second cut was deeper. She watched a thin trickle of blood drip off her arm onto the fence. By the third cut, her dark mood faded, replaced by the sharp reality of physical pain blocking out everything else. Her knife was poised for the fourth cut when her cell phone rang.

She shifted the knife to her other hand and pulled out the phone. If it was her mother, she wasn't answering. She recognized the number and debated ignoring it, but curiosity won out and she accepted the call.

"Tori?"

She recognized Ashley's voice, but instead of her earlier frustration, she was relieved to have someone to talk to. "What's up?" Cradling the phone between her ear and shoulder, she cleaned off her knife and stuck it back in her pocket.

"I'm at the barn. Something's wrong with Saxon."

Tori jumped off the fence. "What do you mean?"

"He keeps kicking his stomach."

"Shit. I'll be there in ten minutes." She hung up and ran to her car. As she drove, she rolled down her shirtsleeve to cover the cuts. Her mind raced through different ideas on what could be wrong with Saxon. Had he gotten injured during the beach ride? He couldn't have, she'd cantered in the arena afterward. She didn't remember much of that ride, she'd been too angry at her mother and Ashley at the time. After the ride he'd seemed fine. She remembered putting him back in his stable and feeding him.

She seemed to take forever before she pulled into the dirt path to the stable parking lot. Her car headlights reflected off the back of Ashley's truck, and she wondered why Ashley was even at the stable so long after sunset. There was enough spill-over from the neighboring streetlights to see her way around the barn yard to Saxon's stable. She made out one shadowed figure leaning against the stable fence.

Ashley turned to her. "He's nipped and kicked at his stomach five times since I called you. I think he's in a lot of pain."

Tori ducked through the fence. Saxon moved his hind quarters away from her as she approached. "Easy, now." She rubbed his face, then studied his body, wishing she had a flashlight. She took a step back when he kicked at his stomach with his hind leg.

"Do you think it's colic?" Ashley asked.

Shit. Saxon pulled away from her. She backed out of the small stable as he kicked at his stomach again. Safely outside the fence, she pulled out her cell phone and keyed in the one speed-dial number she knew could help her horse. "Dad? Something's wrong with Saxon. I think he might be colicing."

"Okay, I'll be there in twenty minutes. Take any food he's got away from him and then just keep a safe distance from him."

She stepped back into the stable, gathered all the remaining hay, and tossed it over the fence. Saxon didn't pay any attention to her. She was tempted to approach him, but her father's warning stayed with her, and she crawled through the fence again to stand next to Ashley. "I don't know why you're here so late, but thanks for calling."

Ashley patted her back pocket. "I left my wallet in my tack room. Makes it hard to buy dinner without it."

"Sorry, I've kept you from dinner. You don't have to wait around with me. My dad's a vet, and he's on his way."

"I'll stay."

Ashley put her hand on Tori's arm, and Tori pulled away, wincing.

"What's wrong?" Ashley saw a dark stain on the shirtsleeve. "You're bleeding!"

Tori covered the patch with her other hand. She couldn't let her father see what she'd done. He'd caught her cutting before and made her see a counselor for a month. She didn't want to deal with that again but even worse, she didn't want to see the disappointment on his face if he knew she was still doing it. She looked between Saxon, who was up and pacing again, and Ashley and made up her mind. "I need your help. I have a jacket in the car but I don't want to leave Saxon. Can you get it for me?"

"Okay. I've got a first aid kit in my truck."

"I don't need that."

Ashley pointed to Tori's bloodstained sleeve. "You must need to hide that from your father or you wouldn't need the jacket, and you need me to keep my mouth shut about it. So you'll take the Band-Aids like a good dyke and take care of that cut." Ashley held out her hand while Tori dug the keys out of her pocket and handed them over.

As she watched Ashley disappear into the darkness, she wasn't sure if she should feel insulted for being treated like a kid, or relieved that Ashley was willing to keep her secret. Maybe Ashley saw it as an even trade, Tori kept her secret about the abortion, and Ashley would never mention the cutting again. It was a bargain she could live with.

A bobbing light made its way down the path from the parking lot, and Tori felt a moment's panic that her father had arrived already. She folded her arms to hide her sleeve, but relaxed when she realized it was just Ashley with a flashlight coming toward her.

Ashley tossed her the jacket. "Here, but we take care of your arm first." She put the first aid kit on the ground, flicked it open, and shone the flashlight over the contents. A small stack of Band-Aids took up one corner, while the rest of the kit had a variety of gauzes, tape, miscellaneous ointments, and what looked like a shoulder sling.

"Let's see what we've got here." Ashley reached for Tori's arm.

Tori pulled back. No one had ever seen her cuts before, not this fresh. They were a private pain. She looked into Ashley's eyes, not knowing how to react or how to explain herself.

"I know what it is." Ashley took a step closer. "Let's just take care of it and get it covered before your father gets here, okay?"

She nodded, raising her injured arm. With a gentle touch, Ashley rolled back the shirtsleeve to expose the three cuts on Tori's forearm. She took a gauze pad and a tiny bottle of saline cleanser out of her kit and soaked the pad. She looked into Tori's eyes. "This might sting a bit." She rinsed off the cuts and the area around them, then cleaned away the patches of congealed blood with the pad.

Tori didn't flinch. She was surprised at how gently Ashley worked. Ashley glanced at her every so often, and Tori gave her a weak smile each time to let her know everything was fine.

With a clean gauze pad over the cuts, held in place by medical tape, Tori rolled down her sleeve and pulled on her jacket to cover the stain. "Good as new."

"Not quite." Ashley repacked her first aid kit and hid it under a bush. "When this is over, you're going to explain what this was all about." She emphasized her words with a tap on Tori's arm, well away from the cuts and glared at her, as if daring her to refuse the demand.

Tori heard Saxon rolling on the ground, but she couldn't do

anything else for him. The night's events crowded around her, each pushing for her full attention. It was more than she could handle. She looked back at Ashley, seeing not just the determination in her face, but something else, something deeper.

"Okay." She knew what she was agreeing to, and it felt right.

A BOUNCING LIGHT approached from the parking area.

"Is that your father?" Ashley asked.

"Yeah." Tori ran to meet him while Ashley waited with Saxon.

Her father handed her a sizable battery-powered spotlight. "How's Saxon doing?"

"He's still standing, but he keeps nipping at his stomach."

They stopped next to Ashley.

"Hi, I'm Ed. You must be Tori's friend," he said.

"Ashley." She shook his hand.

"Sorry," Tori said, a bit embarrassed that she hadn't introduced them. "Ashley found Saxon like this."

Tori shone the light on Saxon as he kicked his stomach again. Her father stepped up to the fence to get a good view of Saxon.

"How long has he been this way?" He rummaged through his medical bag and pulled out a carton containing a fresh syringe.

Ashley glanced at her watch. It was past nine o'clock. "At least an hour."

He nodded, filling the syringe from a bottle. "I'll give him a dose of Banamine first to lessen the pain, then I can evaluate the problem. That will take a little time to kick in. Meanwhile, has there been any change in his diet?"

Tori leaned against the fence, still holding the light on Saxon. "No. He gets two flakes of alfalfa hay in the mornings and evenings, and usually some grain and supplements, but I didn't feed him that today."

Her father stepped into the stable to administer the medicine.

Ashley leaned closer to her and whispered, "Shouldn't you tell him about feeding Saxon right after exercise?"

She flinched. "Um, maybe, if he can't figure out what's wrong." She forgot she'd fed him twice his normal amount, the hay she gave him right after exercise and the normal two flakes in his stable. Overfeeding right after exercise must have led to Saxon's current state. Why was she such a screw-up all the time?

It took an hour for the medication to start helping Saxon, an hour where she kept up a nervous banter about everything but Saxon's latest feeding. Her father might understand the mistake, but he'd tell her mother, and then she'd have to hear about how irresponsible and hopeless she was.

"Okay, let's see what the problem is." Her father grabbed a stethoscope and thermometer and headed back into the stable. After taking Saxon's temperature, he spent a long time listening to the horse's stomach through the stethoscope.

He stepped out of the stable. "The good news is that his heart rate is only mildly elevated and his temperature is normal. He's also got a lot of sound in his gut."

"Is that good or bad?" Tori asked.

He stooped to dig through his medical bag. "Very good. It means his gut isn't twisted, which is the worst kind of colic." He pulled out more medication and gave Saxon another injection. The horse remained relaxed while he returned to Tori and Ashley. "That should help alleviate the type of colic he has. Now we sit and wait."

They'd be watching Saxon for signs of improvement for the next few hours. Tori's stomach rumbled a quiet protest, but she wasn't going to leave just to feed it, not until she knew Saxon was going to be okay. Ashley didn't look like she was leaving either. Tori would thank her for that later, when Saxon was okay.

He had to be okay.

Chapter 9

TORI STRETCHED OUT on the hood of her car and stared up into the leafless trees. She wore faded jeans torn at both knees and a pair of muddy work boots. And, of course, the knife, because that's what this little hike with Ashley was going to be about.

Ashley's truck rumbled into the trail head parking lot twenty minutes late and parked next to Tori. She wore a hooded sweatshirt with Santa Clara University written across her chest in block letters. *Hell of a nice chest, too*, Tori thought.

"Sorry I'm late," Ashley said.

Tori hopped off her car. "It's okay. It's better to be here than at home."

"Your mother is still ticked off about the colic episode?"

"She's 'worried' about me." Tori shrugged. "It's all part of her 'irresponsible, directionless, waste-of-time daughter' approach to parenting. She'll be writing a how-to manual soon, I'm sure."

Tori led the way up a steep, muddy path that got more slippery in the leaf-covered patches. Within a few minutes, they lost sight of the parking lot and all other evidence of civilization, except the constant whir of traffic from the distant highway. Patches of the forest floor were thick with green, signaling the presence of a stream. They walked across one stream, using two weathered slats of wood as a bridge. Ferns crowded the banks on either side of the trickling water, the soothing sound adding to the pleasant chirps of birds overhead.

Tori didn't leave much of an opportunity for conversation as they climbed the trail. She'd promised to talk to Ashley about the cutting, but she didn't promise to make it easy. At each fork in the trail, she chose the steeper option. Eventually, she ran out of options, as the forest opened up into a small meadow surrounded by towering redwoods.

Ashley paused at the edge of the trees. "It's gorgeous."

Tori grinned, slowing down to let Ashley walk beside her. "It's a good spot to hide. If you're quiet enough, sometimes the deer wander in without even noticing you."

Ashley hopped on a felled redwood trunk. Her boots just skimmed the ground from where she sat. "Come join me." She patted the tree trunk.

Tori sat next to her and scraped at the moss growing over the weathered bark.

"Why do you cut?"

Tori's hand froze over the moss she was picking at, and she crossed her arms. "Different reasons."

"Pick one."

She glared at Ashley. "Keisha."

"Ex-girlfriend?"

"Ex-sister."

Ashley blinked a couple of times. "You're going to have to explain that one. How does someone become an ex-sister?"

"She dropped dead." Tori stared off at the trees. She hadn't planned on being so blunt about it. When she rehearsed it in her head, it was a lot less sarcastic.

"Oh, sorry. Was she older or younger than you?"

"She was thirty."

"Twelve years older than you? That's a big gap."

"She was my half-sister." She let out a snort. "And my mother's favorite. Perfect Keisha. Straight, and femme, and all-black. Everything I'm not."

Ashley patted her arm and smiled. "I for one am very glad you're not straight and not femme, but you are black, right? I mean I didn't get that wrong, did I?"

"Not black enough for my mother." It was like an express train to Bitterland, and she was the sole rider. "I never got on with her side of the family, not like Keisha did." She pointed at her hair. "I never got this straightened, relaxed, hot-ironed, or anything. I used to have to go with them up to Oakland to visit Keisha's dad and get our hair done by one of my aunts. When I was seven, I cut all my hair off with the kitchen scissors. My mother was so embarrassed she left me at home with my dad."

Ashley brushed back the curls that Tori had tugged across her forehead. "I love your hair, it's gorgeous."

She blushed, and Ashley laughed. "Big bad Tori is all embarrassed now because I complimented her."

"Yeah, yeah."

"How did straightened hair make Keisha blacker than you?"

Tori shrugged. "It's more than just the hair. Keisha grew up in Oakland where the rest of my mom's family lives. We lived down here by the time I came along. I spent more time with my dad's family in Santa Clara. I didn't grow up feeling black, not the way she did."

"Why would your mother rate your blackness or whatever? She married a white guy."

Tori just shrugged. It wasn't something she could explain. Keisha was all black, and she was half and half. It just added to how she'd never be enough for her mother.

"When did Keisha die?"

Tori rubbed her palms against the tree, wearing away the moss cover. They were steaming through Bitterland and about to crash at the Tori's-a-Psycho train stop. "Back in May. She had cervical cancer."

Ashley paled. "What about chemo? Didn't that help?"

"She was too far advanced by the time it was diagnosed. They still made her go through chemo and radiation, but it just made her sicker." Tori closed her eyes. She could still remember how frail Keisha felt when she'd helped her get in and out of bed. It wasn't a memory she wanted to bring back.

"So that's why you cut?"

She scraped her palms against the exposed tree bark, breaking off the looser pieces. "That's not the only reason."

"What's the other reason?"

"Robyn."

"Not another ex-sister?"

"Ex-girlfriend. The one I wasn't gay enough for."

"I've been accused of that because I'm bisexual, but you seem one hundred percent dyke to me."

Tori broke off a piece of the tree bark and fiddled with it. "I'm not out, not like you and Robyn."

"So? I mean being out makes it easier to pick up chicks, but otherwise, who cares?"

"She cared. Enough to break up with me when Keisha died. I wouldn't bring her to the funeral with me." There was another memory she didn't want to resurface. She scraped the bark across her palm. It didn't work as well as the knife, but it was better than nothing.

"She's an asshole."

Tori looked up with a half grin. "You form some fast opinions."

"You don't think she's an asshole?"

She went back to her piece of bark. One part was abrasive enough to draw blood. Ashley grabbed her hand and flipped it over to expose the dirty, red cuts in the palm.

"Why?"

She felt the start of tears as she held Ashley's gaze. "It's a cleaner pain to deal with. It's easier."

"This isn't clean." Ashley held her palm in one hand, pulled out a fast-food napkin from her jacket pocket with her other hand. It wasn't the most sanitary thing in the world, but neither was the bark Tori had used to make the cut.

Ashley cupped her palm between her hands. "You need to stop this. She's not worth it, and neither is competing with your dead sister."

"Easier said than done."

Ashley let go of her injured hand. "Give me the bark."

Tori dropped the bark in Ashley's outstretched hand.

"What did you use on your arm the other day?"

She pulled out the knife from her back pocket.

"Pearl handled? That's kind of girlie for you, don't you think?"

"I stole it from Keisha." She ran a finger over the handle. It didn't have the shine it used to have, but she kept the edge sharp.

Ashley let out a long sigh. "So you cut with a knife you stole from Keisha."

"A month before she died. Her dad gave it to her when she was a kid." Tori fiddled with the knife, but didn't open it.

"Shit. How much guilt can you wrap up in one little blade?" Ashley held out her hand. "Give it to me."

Tori hesitated. She shouldn't have stolen the knife to begin with. She thought Keisha would notice and shout at her, but she never did. She died instead.

She opened her palm and held out the knife.

Ashley grabbed it and stuffed it in her jacket pocket. "I didn't think you'd accept my wonder-treatment."

"If I get caught cutting, my parents will toss me at a psychologist again. Your wonder-treatment has better office hours than my last therapist."

"And I'm better looking."

Tori laughed. "And you're better looking."

"Okay, as your new wonder-therapist, I'm keeping the knife until you get a better grip on your sister's death. And forget about your ex-bitch."

Tori leaned closer and whispered, "You're bordering on dominatrix, you know that?"

"Some girls like that." Ashley stood up and offered her a hand. "Now take me back to civilization before I show you just how much of a dom I can be."

Tori didn't budge. "Not until you make with some confessions about yourself. You know all my dirty secrets. Time to share some of your own."

"My life's an open book."

"Do you have any lingering issues from, you know, the abortion?" Tori knew it was the last thing Ashley wanted to talk about, but she didn't get to keep everything to herself after dragging Tori's story from her.

Ashley crossed her arms. "I don't know. Most of the time it's like it never happened. Other times I think I have a stamp on my forehead that screams stupid slut."

Tori's eyebrows shot up. "That's harsh. No one would think that if they knew."

"You don't know my uncles. They've said that and worse about my mother. She had her first abortion when she was younger than I am."

"What about your grandfather? He's okay with it, isn't he?"

Ashley dug her heel into the matted leaves. "I haven't told him."

"Oh."

Ashley looked up. "It's not that I want to hide it or anything, but he's already got too much going on. He's got cancer."

Cancer. Tori stood up and took Ashley's hand. "Why didn't you tell me? How bad is it?"

Ashley patted her cheek. "You really are a doll, you know that? The surgery went well, but there were more small tumors than they thought. He's going through chemo now and it's taking a lot out of him."

"Keisha didn't take well to it, either. It affects some people more than others."

"Yeah, I guess. Can we head back now?"

Tori had stifled talk about Keisha plenty of times in the past to recognize Ashley wanted to drop the subject. The walk back down the muddy trail was easier than the hike up. Tori didn't extricate her hand from Ashley's, and Ashley didn't try to let go. *Friends hold hands sometimes*, she told herself, even as she realized she wanted more. What they had right now was good, though. She wasn't going to screw it up.

TORI RODE SAXON in a slow circle around Michelle and Tank Girl in the round pen. Tank Girl was in full bridle and saddle, staying stationary despite keeping a keen eye on Saxon as he walked by.

"Okay, ease into a trot and let's see how she behaves," Michelle said.

She gave Saxon a nudge with her heels, and he sped up into a slow trot. Tank Girl pivoted to watch him, but Michelle kept her from moving any further.

"She doesn't trust him," Ashley said, watching from just outside the pen.

Tori sped up her trot. "He's a gelding, what's he going to do?"

"A dude's a dude," Ashley said, and Tori laughed, not expecting such insight from a bisexual woman. Then again, Ashley was full of the unexpected. When Michelle asked for another rider for today's lesson, Ashley offered Tori's services instead of riding Apostle herself. Things were different after the hike.

Saxon lengthened his trot, relaxing into the exercise as she completed another circle around Tank Girl. Michelle urged Tank Girl into a slow walk in the opposite direction around the pen.

Tori's newest cuts itched. Ashley had acted like a nurse in training, cleaning out the dirt from the bark before taping another gauze pad on her. If this kept up, Tori would need to buy her a new first aid kit.

She hadn't cut herself at all since then. In her less-honest moments, she told herself it was because it was nearly Christmas, and she had no school and no responsibilities besides barn work and pizza delivery. Giving Ashley a quick glance on her way by, she knew that was just an excuse. Every morning when she got dressed and every night, she remembered where her pocket knife was and that was enough so far to keep her in line. Hell, she hadn't even had a drink all week.

"Okay, bring him back down to a walk and let's see if she'll walk beside him." Michelle and Tank Girl made a narrow inner circle around the pen while Tori slowed Saxon and reversed direction. As she approached them from behind, Tank Girl flattened her ears and tried to kick Saxon with her back legs.

"That's not very nice." Michelle turned Tank Girl in a tight circle until she calmed down and started listening again. "Let's try that again, only this time I'll walk her up to Saxon."

Tori signaled Saxon into a slow walk, keeping to the outer edge of the pen. Michelle and Tank Girl approached from the rear and this time, Tank Girl behaved herself, riding beside Saxon as if it they were best buddies.

"Now she likes him," Ashley said.

"A chick's a chick," Tori said.

Ashley laughed. "We both know chicks don't always go for the dudes."

Tori wasn't bothered by the innuendo since everyone at the stable knew about her and Robyn. The only people she wasn't out to were her own family.

Michelle ended the lesson, and Ashley led her horse back to her stable. Tori took advantage of the empty round pen to canter for another few minutes before taking Saxon back to his stable for a groom. When she was done, she found Ashley and Michelle sitting at the picnic table, and Michelle was laughing so hard there were tears in her eyes.

"What's so funny?" she asked, taking a seat next to Ashley but not close enough to suggest, well, anything.

Michelle wiped at her eyes. "Ashley was just telling me about her favorite part of the holiday season."

Ashley crossed her arms. "I like Christmas carols, so what?"

"Yeah, but you're not talking about 'Jingle Bells' and 'Grandma Got Run Over by a Reindeer.'"

Ashley let out an exasperated sigh. "Those aren't Christmas carols, they're just songs."

"So what do you like?" Tori asked, still not sure what was so funny.

"I like to go caroling." Ashley glared at her as if defying her to laugh about it.

"So like the religious songs, 'Silent Night' and all that?" Tori shrugged. "That's cool. I like them better, too."

Michelle threw up her hands. "Peas in a pod, you two. I'm out of here before you try to rope me into going to church or something." She hopped off the bench and went back to her office.

Ashley grabbed Tori's arm. "That's a great idea!"

"What is?"

"Church. Come to church with me on Thursday. They're doing a special Christmas caroling service."

She almost laughed but she saw the intensity in Ashley's eyes. "I didn't know you went to church."

Ashley let go of her arm. "Not all the time, but you know, for Christmas and Easter." She gave Tori a sly grin. "And when I feel the need to confess a few sins."

"Right. So that would be pretty much every Sunday, then."

"You want to give me something to confess about this week?" Ashley leaned closer, bouncing her eyebrows in such a comical manner that Tori knew she wasn't really flirting.

She'd been wishing Ashley would drop the flirt act for months and now that she had, she felt disappointed. How fickle was that?

"Come on, it'll be fun."

"The sinning or the caroling?" Tori asked.

"Both, but let's just go with the caroling for now."

She shrugged. "Okay."

"Great." Ashley gave Tori a bear hug. Tori was aware of every place their bodies touched, from the feel of Ashley's arms around her to the press of Ashley's chest against hers. She stroked Ashley's back and didn't even know at what point she hugged Ashley back, but she knew she didn't want to stop.

Ashley cupped her cheek and stroked it lightly with her thumb. "You're adorable when you blush."

Tori brushed her hand away. "And you're an impossible tease."

Ashley gave her a crooked smile. "Oh, I'm possible, definitely possible."

"That's not what I meant."

Ashley laughed. "I know, I know. Now back to Thursday. It's my grandfather's church so you don't have to worry about me being impossible. We'll be chaperoned for the evening."

That twinge of disappointment popped up again, and Tori gave up trying to squelch it. So what if she liked Ashley? Nothing would happen anyway. Ashley was an obvious player, and Tori didn't share well with others. Still, it felt good to think someone besides Robyn was hot. And Ashley was definitely hot.

"Are you listening?"

"Yeah, I am. So how do I get to your grandfather's place?"

TORI STOOD ON Ashley's porch and straightened her tie. She'd shocked her mother by ironing her white tailored shirt and black jeans, but had kept the tie hidden. She didn't want to push her mother over the edge. Her mother had even complimented her on her way out. Maybe they were both feeling that Christmas spirit.

She rang the doorbell. Ashley stepped out a moment later.

"Hey." Tori swept her gaze over Ashley. They were dressed almost identically. If she looked good, Ashley looked hot.

"Am I dressed okay?" she asked.

"Definitely okay."

Ashley stepped outside and turned to lock the door, giving Tori a moment to recover. If this had been a real date, she could have brought Ashley flowers or something. She stomped down on her wayward thoughts. They were only feeding her embarrassing blush.

"How far is the church?" she asked.

Ashley had a shaky smile on her face. "About five miles, not too far."

"Is your grandfather coming?"

"No, he's not feeling well."

"Oh, sorry. Do you need to stay home with him?"

"He all but threw me out. Stubborn bastard."

"I know where you get it from, now." She rushed back to her car and opened the passenger door, grinning sheepishly. "Mind if I drive?"

"You're not going to make this easy, are you?" Ashley slid into the passenger seat.

"What?" Tori hesitated in closing the door for her.

Ashley shook her head. "That's the beauty of it all, Tori Kahl. You haven't a clue. Close the door, Miss Chivalry, and let's get going."

The church was smaller than Tori expected. A congregation of less than thirty people sat scattered across the pews, small pockets of family mixed with a solitary senior here and there.

It was nothing like the Baptist church her mother dragged them to on Christmas and Easter. The last time she'd been there was for Keisha's funeral. Then it was filled with aunts, uncles, and cousins who poured out of Oakland to mourn for her sister in ways more vocal than Tori ever could.

She'd never go back to that church.

Her hand itched for the knife that used to be in her back pocket. She glanced at Ashley beside her, who sang the first Christmas carol in a sweet, imperfect voice. It didn't seem to bother Ashley that she went off-tune now and then.

Tori let the music smother her morbid thoughts. The service wasn't really a service at all, but more an excuse for singing their favorite songs. The church choir directed the music, but the people in the pews gave it life. She joined in on the more popular songs near the end.

"What did you think?" Ashley asked when it was over and they drifted out of the pews with the rest of the congregation.

"What happened to 'Grandma Got Run Over by a Reindeer'?"

Ashley elbowed her in the ribs.

"Okay, okay. It was good."

"See, now it didn't hurt to go to church, did it?"

Tori rubbed her side. "I guess."

"Oh, spare me the dramatics." Ashley looped her hands

around Tori's arm as they walked to the parking lot. Tori didn't pull away until they were back at the car, then she opened Ashley's door for her again.

Ashley paused, standing just inches away from Tori. She slipped Tori's tie between her fingers. "You look hot tonight."

Tori was close enough to feel Ashley's warm breath. She extracted her tie and held Ashley's hand instead. "So do you."

If Ashley made a move, she wouldn't turn her down. Ashley didn't, though. She squirmed into the passenger seat instead, and Tori shut her door. Tori slid into the driver's seat and brushed away her fantasies of what it would be like between them.

The drive home went faster than she would have liked, but she couldn't think of a way to extend the evening. They stood on Ashley's front porch in an awkward silence.

"Do you want to come inside?"

Tori hesitated. "Isn't your grandfather sick? He's probably not up for company."

Ashley sighed. "Yeah, I guess you're right."

Tori wished she'd kept her big mouth shut. Maybe her grandfather was already in bed? Maybe he wouldn't care? She looked at Ashley. Was that regret in her eyes or just her own wishful thinking?

"I had a good night."

"Me, too." Tori shuffled from foot to foot. "I never did say thank you, by the way."

"For?"

Tori looked up. Ashley's eyes reflected the porch light that her grandfather had left on for them. "For listening to me the other day. For taking the knife."

Ashley stepped closer and took her hand. "That's what friends are for."

Tori stared down at their hands. If she shifted a couple of inches, they'd be in kissing range.

Ashley lifted Tori's chin and gazed into her eyes. She pointed up. "You can't blame me for this one."

Tori glanced up. "Mistletoe?"

Ashley nodded, licking her lips as she cupped Tori's face. "Can't break with tradition."

Tori didn't pull back. Her eyes drifted shut just a moment after Ashley closed her eyes. Ashley's lips brushed hers in what started as a light kiss, but those soft, full lips drew her in. She lost all sense of time.

The sound of a fire siren in the distance broke the spell of the mistletoe. She eased out of the kiss. Ashley stood in the circle of her arms. She was breathless and more than a little unsure of herself. Her pulse raced, and she felt the pull of Ashley's touch deep inside her. She wanted more of this, a whole damn lot more, and that scared her.

She took a slow step backward. "I should probably get going." She brushed back loose strands of Ashley's hair.

Ashley kissed her hand and let it go. "I'm stuck at my uncle's house for Christmas. You better text me."

"I will."

Ashley stood on the porch and waved as Tori drove away. Where was she going with all this? She could think of a dozen reasons why she should stay away from Ashley. With the memory of their kiss still lingering on her lips, none of the reasons seemed enough to keep her from wanting more.

Chapter 10

TORI TORE OPEN the letter from De Anza College. At the bottom of her string of B's and C's was her history grade. It was a C minus. "Woot!" She got okay grades without Robyn's help for the first time since Keisha's illness. That was better than all the rest of her Christmas presents combined.

Her mother shuffled into the kitchen in her slippers. "Good news, I take it?" Her voice was raspy from the onset of a cold.

"I passed all my classes."

"Passed?" Her mother held out her hand. "Let's see it."

She was in college now. She didn't need to have her grades scrutinized by her parents anymore, but she was happy with them. She handed the report over.

Her mother's gaze slammed to a halt right where Tori expected her to. "That's the best you could do in History?"

She took the paper and stuffed it in her back pocket. "I could have done better, but then you'd have nothing to bitch about, would you?"

"Don't swear at me, Tori." Her mother scowled as if she expected her to cower and apologize.

As if she ever did. "Come on, if I didn't give you a sacrificial grade, you'd be disappointed."

"My only disappointment is that you still haven't matured, even in college. You have no declared major, no motivation, and no direction in your life. How long do you think you can keep floating through like this? Do you want to end up like your cousin, Dinea?"

Dinea, the black sheep of the black family, and her mother's worst nightmare, if the number of times she threw that name at Tori counted. Dinea had slipped from the middle-class Oakland neighborhood where Tori's aunt and uncle lived to one of the worst of the worst areas of the city. She'd had two abortions before she was seventeen and who knows how many after she'd left home.

"Trust me, Mom, I don't have Dinea's problems." She grabbed her jacket and ran out the back door before she got whipped with more of her mother's caustic attitude. Of course her grades wouldn't be good enough. She wasn't smart like her brother, or driven into an early grave like Keisha. Nope. She was the black sheep of this family, the only thing she was black enough for her mother.

Her mother's head popped out the back door. "Don't forget to pick up a birthday present for Jerome," she rasped.

Maybe her mother's cold would turn to pneumonia. Tori stuffed her hands in her pockets, searching for the one thing she was missing and wanting right now, her knife. She dug out her keys instead and hopped in her car. The knife was gone, but not the urge to use it. She gunned the engine, screeched out of the driveway, and headed down the hill. She had no plan on where she was going besides away from her mother.

She parked at a turnout, pulled out her cell phone, and thumbed in a text message to Ashley. *Where are you?*

She got back on the road and continued down the hill. Her cell phone belted out a half-dozen notes of Outkast's latest song before the mountain road straightened out. She flipped the phone open and read Ashley's response.

At the barn.

She knew where she wanted to go now.

The drive to the barn gave her time to calm down. The urge to cut disappeared by the time she parked beside Ashley's truck. She found Ashley in Tank Girl's stable swearing at her horse. The reason was obvious. Tori laughed so hard she had tears in her eyes.

Ashley glared at her. "It's not funny. How the hell do I get her out?"

Tank Girl stood with her front legs inside her water trough. Ashley was soaked from Tank Girl's attempts to stomp her way back out, but the trough's high rim kept her trapped.

Tori stifled her laughter for Ashley's sake. "At least she's not panicking."

"For now."

Tori patted Tank Girl's face. "Next time, just ask your owner when you want a bath."

"Excuse me, Captain Sarcastic. Do you have any bright ideas or did you come here just to be another pain in my ass?"

Someone was in a bad mood. "Sorry." Tori walked around the horse. "You tried backing her up?"

"Yes. She's not lifting her legs high enough. I tried lifting them higher myself, but she won't back up if I have one of her legs up."

"What if you try that again and I'll push her back?"

Ashley yanked her hair back into a ponytail. "As if I'm not wet enough already."

"Okay, we'll let the water out first, then try it again." Tori pulled the cap off the drain plug and stepped back. Water gushed out of the trough. They waited until it turned to a trickle.

She stood in front of Tank Girl. "Ready?"

Ashley lifted Tank Girl's front leg in answer.

Tori clicked her tongue and pushed. "Come on, girl, back up."

Tank Girl didn't budge.

"Shit stupid horse!" Ashley slapped her side. Tank Girl pulled her leg free of Ashley's one-handed grip and bucked. Ashley and Tori both jumped out of the way. The empty water trough tipped, frightening Tank Girl into another series of bucks that eventually set her free.

"Well, that worked," Tori said.

"About time something did." Ashley smacked Tank Girl on the side to get her out of the way, then lifted the water trough back up.

Tori pulled over the water hose and started filling the trough. "Is anything else wrong?"

Ashley leaned against the paddock fence and stared at the ground. "No, nothing's wrong."

"That's not very convincing."

"I'm fine." Ashley took another yank at her ponytail to pull back stray hairs. "I need to finish mucking out." She walked into the stable.

And just like that, Ashley locked her out. Tori's imagination took over. Was Ashley having girl problems or boy problems with someone else?

She didn't bother with good-bye. She dropped the hose into the trough and walked away. On the way to her car, she pulled out her cell phone and punched in the speed-dial number for Jackie.

"YOU WERE BETTER off with Robyn," Jackie said between hiccups.

Tori scratched at the label of her beer bottle. "Maybe." The scraps of paper fell on Jackie's kitchen table.

"She was asking about you the other day, you know."

"Robyn? What did you tell her?" And why was Jackie talking to her ex-girlfriend anyway? Where was the loyalty?

"I told her you had a hot new girlfriend."

"Oh." Maybe only part of a new girlfriend if Ashley was seeing other people.

"Maybe I should have kept my mouth shut. She sounded kind of interested in seeing you again."

Tori dropped her head into her hands. She didn't have the patience for the way her thoughts grasped at the idea that Robyn might take her back. It was stupid. She was stupid. "I'm going home." She reached for her keys on the kitchen table but Jackie got them first.

Jackie dangled the keys just out of reach. "Are you sure you can drive?"

She finished off her last beer and stood up. The room did an unnecessary spin but didn't throw off her step when she made a grab for her keys. "After only two beers? Yeah."

"More like four." Jackie tried to keep the keys from her, but being a good foot shorter, the effort was wasted.

She pocketed her keys. "Nice try."

"You could hang out for a couple of hours. It's only three o'clock."

"I've got to get home for my brother's birthday."

She got in her car and blasted the music as she drove from Jackie's parent's house in San Jose to the Santa Cruz Mountains. The air was cold, but not cold enough to turn the steady rain to snow. She drove too fast for her road, but was conscientious enough to hit the brakes before the driveway wall got in the way. She was in the house and staring at Jerome in the living room when she remembered the one errand she needed to do today. "Shit."

Jerome glanced at her from the sofa. "Nice to see you too, butthead."

She walked to him and ruffled his hair in just the way she knew he hated. He pulled away with a jerk and a scowl. She sat down next to him, laughing hysterically.

"What's your issue?" He leaned in and sniffed her, then backed away. "You'd better change before Mom sees you."

She took a whiff of herself. "That bad?"

"Oh yeah. And brush your teeth or something. You smell like the kitchen after Dad's poker night."

Stale beer and cigarettes. She hadn't smoked, but Jackie lit up a few times. She showered and brushed her teeth, then swirled some mouthwash for good measure before returning downstairs.

"Better?" she asked, parading in front of Jerome's TV viewing.

"Less obvious, anyway," he said, shoving her out of his way.

The back door opened, and her mother came in with bags of party supplies dangling from each arm. "A little help here." She kicked the door shut and walked to the kitchen table.

Tori went outside to retrieve the rest of the bags and the sheet cake with "Happy Birthday" sprawled across it in Jerome's favorite colors. Managing to balance it all in her arms without dumping the cake got her a disapproving frown from her mother.

"Next time, make two trips."

She dropped the bags on the floor and slid the cake on the kitchen counter before her mother grabbed her elbow.

"Did you get him a present?"

Tori shrugged. "Not yet."

Her mother rolled her eyes as Jerome walked in to see his cake. "You, get out of the kitchen," she said to him, and to Tori, "You've got an hour. Go get his present."

Jerome blanched. "That's okay, she doesn't have to get it today."

"Yes, she does."

"Fine." Tori stomped out of the house without grabbing a jacket. The rain attacked her in windy gusts on the way to her car. She gunned the engine extra hard to piss off her mother before squealing out of the driveway.

Perfect Jerome needed the perfect present for his perfect party. She scowled through the rain sheeting across her windscreen, but she wasn't angry at her brother. They got on well most of the time, and he covered for her whenever he could.

The downpour sent small streams of water across the road and the wind tore the last remnants of leaves from the trees. She just wanted to get this stupid errand over with. Her back tires slid out behind her on a narrow switchback. She jammed the steering wheel to the side to compensate for the skid. Her car spun out of control instead. She heard it grind against a tree as she slammed on the breaks and her head bounced off the back of the car seat. She was hyperventilating by the time the car came to a stop in a ditch by the roadside.

The wipers continued their methodical swish back and forth across the windscreen. She leaned back in the seat and closed her eyes, counting each inhale and exhale until her breathing slowed. What had gone wrong? She wasn't even sure how she lost control of the car. She was lucky to end in a ditch instead of tumbling down one of the steeper slopes along the road.

She opened her eyes. Matted leaves stuck to the hood. Besides the steady beat of the wipers, she heard nothing else. The engine had stopped or died during the crash. She unbuckled and tried to open the door, but it resisted. She crawled to the passenger side and got out. The rain came in heavy drops as she stepped around the car and surveyed the damage. She'd lost one headlight and had a major dent in the driver's door and front fender. That must have been the scraping noise she heard. She cleared the debris off her hood and saw a few more scratches, but nothing too bad. Still, she'd never get the car out of the ditch on her own, even if it did start up again.

Another car approached. She panicked, hiding in the woods below the ditch. If the police came, she'd be caught for driving drunk. The car slowed down, and she ran deeper into the woods, then angled upslope. It couldn't be more than a couple of miles to her home. Better to face a pissed off mother than a cop who'd take her license away for months.

The walk home took more than an hour, giving her plenty of time to sober up and feel the effects of the crash. Her neck and her left elbow hurt. She must have banged it on the door at some point. She also had a sore spot to match her seatbelt. She didn't know if her knee hurt from the car or from the three times she slid down the slippery slope during her escape hike.

She had plenty of time to mull over her over-active jealousy gene, too. She could have just accepted that Ashley had a bad day, but no, she had to assume the worst. See where that got her.

By the time she got to her driveway, she was a wet, muddy, aching mess. She couldn't even unlock the door because she'd left her keys in the ignition. She rang the bell and waited for the inevitable bitchfest.

Jerome opened the back door, his eyes widening as he looked her over. "Shit, what happened to you?"

"Language, Jerome." Their mother's voice scraped like the caw of a crow.

Not dead of pneumonia yet, Tori thought as she stepped

inside. She had no idea what she looked like, besides wet and dirty, but her mother was off the sofa in a flash and coming at her with eyes as wide as Jerome's.

"I know, I'm getting the kitchen muddy," Tori said.

"Shit, what *did* happen to you?" her mother said.

"Nothing." She tried to kick off her boots. When they wouldn't budge, she remembered having to tie them properly to keep from tripping so much in the woods. She bent down to untie them, but her left knee refused to cooperate. Her mother grabbed her arm, the injured one. She pulled back, almost losing her balance.

"Nothing, my ass, what happened?" Her mother held her other arm, more gingerly this time, to help her sit.

"Language, Mother," she said, bending her one good knee to untie her boots.

"Stuff the sarcasm and tell me how you got hurt."

She couldn't stand her mother's worried expression so she stared at her muddy boots, dripping on the kitchen tiles. "The car skidded in the rain, and I ended up in a ditch."

Her mother glanced out the window and then back at her. "You left the car there?"

"I couldn't get it out of the ditch on my own." She left out the drunken panic part. She glanced at Jerome and knew he guessed the truth.

"Why didn't you just call?" Her mother studied her from her wet head to muddy boots. "What hurts?"

Tori rolled her neck, but couldn't complete the motion without wincing in pain. "Besides the neck, elbow, and knee, nothing."

Her mother grabbed her keys. "Jerome, call your dad, tell him about the car and tell him I'm taking Tori to the emergency room."

"I don't need the emergency room." Her voice had no real fight left in it.

"Hush up. You don't know what you need." Her mother was already in the foyer closet, grabbing her rain coat.

Tori stood up, slowly. "Can I at least get some dry clothes on?"

Her mother paused at the door. "Do you think you can? Do you need help?"

Tori sat back and fought with her laces to get her boot off the injured leg. "At eighteen, I think I can dress myself."

"Wiseass. Hurry up then."

THE BRUISES WEREN'T so good, but the extra attention from Ashley made up for it. Ashley tried to make herself available most times when Tori needed a ride, which was a lot.

Tori's car needed repairs she couldn't afford. The mechanic was a friend of her dad and gave them a good price for the repairs, but it was a low-priority for him. Tori wouldn't see her car for a while. She had to beg a ride to the barn whenever it rained and ride her mountain bike on the other days.

Her latest beg-ride came from Jackie, who was dressed in clothes that screamed "Not suitable for horse barns"—white pants and two-inch heeled suede boots. She stood by while Tori backed the tractor up to the hay barn for the evening feed.

Jackie hopped from foot to foot. "I know I'll regret this, but where's the bathroom around here?"

Tori jumped out of the tractor. "Behind the hay barn."

"Indoor plumbing?"

"Porta-potty."

"Great. If I'm not back in five minutes, send for help." Jackie shivered and walked off toward the sole toilet.

Tori opened the hay barn and walked into the dusty interior to fetch the hay. She poked her head out of the barn and tossed a bale of hay into the tractor's wagon. She saw Ashley emerge from Tank Girl's stable and waved.

Ashley arrived at the hay barn just as Tori piled another bale onto the tractor. "Hey, how are the bruises?"

Tori poked at her ribs. "A little sensitive, but not too bad. My knee's the worst. Makes riding a bike a real pain."

Ashley grinned. "I bet it does. Sorry I couldn't come get you this time."

"That's okay. I've been bumming a lot of rides from you, lately." And stealing a lot of steamy kisses.

"I'm not complaining."

Jackie burst out of the portable toilet. She clung to Tori's arm, making fake barfing noises. "That's the most disgusting place on the planet." She smacked Tori's arm. "Why didn't you warn me?"

Jackie glanced between Tori and Ashley. "Hi, I'm Jackie."

"Um, sorry," Tori said. "This is Ashley."

"Ashley? This is so cool. Tori's told me loads about you."

Ashley gave Tori a questioning glance as she shook Jackie's hand.

This would be a good time to shut up, Jackie. Tori peeled Jackie off her arm. "I didn't say that much."

"Oh, she can't stop talking about you sometimes," Jackie said. Tori elbowed her, but she ignored it. "Hey, we're going to a party after this, do you want to join us?"

Ashley's smile faded. "No thanks. I've got a sick grandfather to visit."

Tori took a step closer to Ashley. "Is he okay?"

"He's got stomach problems."

"Chemo was hard for Keisha, too." Near the end. Tori had never asked how far Iain's cancer had progressed and kicked herself for being so insensitive. She didn't want to drag the full details out of Ashley while Jackie was listening.

"I better go," Ashley said.

"Okay. Text me later about Iain."

Jackie waited until Ashley disappeared before getting her digs in. "So that's the infamous Ashley, eh? Not much for conversation, is she?"

"She's got a lot on her mind." Tori stepped back into the hay barn to end the conversation before Jackie said something to really piss her off.

JACKIE SAT NEXT to Tori while she drove the full tractor to the first pasture. She gripped the sides of the tractor as it bounced along. "How long's this going to take?"

"Twenty minutes for the upper pastures and another twenty to feed each stable."

"Matt better be back to pick us up by then. I don't want to hang around this smell longer than necessary."

Tori wasn't in the mood to cater to Jackie's selfishness. She'd already lost her pizza delivery job because she didn't have access to a car anymore, and now she'd let Ashley go without finding out how sick her grandfather was.

She gunned the engine up the incline to the upper pastures. "You could have gone with him."

"Oh, no I couldn't. He's off on his stupid secret project again. He better not be screwing some other girl."

Tori didn't have a good response to that so she kept quiet. Matt had been mystery boy for months now, telling them only that he had work to do for his uncle. She didn't think he was cheating on Jackie though. One of the reasons she and Matt got along so well was that they both had the same views on relationships—sex comes after love, and you only love one person at a time. Serial dating, Jackie called it, but Tori knew she felt the same way, at least about the sex part.

When Tori stopped the tractor outside the mares' pasture and hopped out, Jackie glared at her. "You don't expect me to help, do you?"

Tori tugged off her first bale, cut the twine holding it together, and tossed the flakes of hay over the fence to the waiting horses. "I wouldn't dream if it." She left two bales for the mares, then drove along to repeat the procedure at the first gelding pasture. After feeding them and the second gelding pasture, she returned to the hay barn to refill the tractor wagon.

Matt showed up as she finished feeding the stabled horses and returned the empty tractor to the hay barn. He trotted over to join them.

"Perfect timing," she said.

Jackie stepped off the tractor and smacked Matt's arm. "Don't ever ditch me in a shitty place like this again."

Matt laughed and scooped her up in his arms. "Never again, fair princess."

Jackie poked him again, but Tori saw that Matt's good mood was infectious. Jackie was giggling as he carried her through the barn yard and back to the parking lot, not putting her down until he had to dig out his car keys. He opened the passenger door and bowed as Jackie got in.

"Now can we finally get to the party?" Jackie asked.

"Not yet." Matt ran around the car and hopped in the driver's seat as Tori scrambled into the back seat.

Jackie glared at him. "Why the hell not?"

He put a finger to his lips. "It's a surprise."

Jackie groaned. "Between the two of you, we'll never make it to this place before all the good liquor is gone."

Matt frowned as he backed his car out of the parking spot. "Do you ever stop thinking about getting drunk?"

"Never." Jackie slouched in her seat as Matt headed to the highway.

Tori recognized the direction he was going. They passed by her house on the way up the mountain.

Jackie wouldn't admit it, but she was getting pulled in by Matt's surprise, sitting up in her seat and looking around. "There's not a lot of road left up here, Matt."

"There's enough." He was grinning from ear to ear by the time he slowed down and pulled into a bumpy, unkempt road. They bounced along for another few minutes as the last remnants of the day's light disappeared and the only thing they could see was what the headlights illuminated. They crawled along a ridged path surrounded by trees, the underbrush cleared just enough to let one car pass. The road opened up to reveal a small A-frame house surrounded by a hard pack of dirt cleared from the surrounding woods.

Matt parked the car and hopped out, leaving the headlights on to showcase the house. "This is it."

Tori and Jackie got out to join him. He unlocked the house and stepped inside. It was dark until he turned on a camp light and held it up. They were in the front room, with a dusty-looking sofa hugging one wall and a wood stove taking up most of the opposite wall. The small house had a kitchen and bathroom on the first floor, along with an overgrown closet that Matt insisted was the laundry room. The living room was separated off by a half wall. A ladder led up to the two tiny bedrooms that made up the loft.

"Well, what do you think?" he asked.

"What's it for?" Jackie asked.

Matt took her hand. "It's for us. My uncle said if I fixed it up, we can stay up here."

Jackie stared at him. "Way up here in the middle of nowhere? Does it even have electricity?"

Matt's eyes reflected the camp light. "There's a generator around back. I just need to fix it up and get fuel, then we're all set."

Tori saw the frightened look in Jackie's eyes and knew things weren't going to go well from here. She backed out of the room. "I'm going to look around the outside a bit."

Neither answered her as she left. She walked around the house, as far as the car's headlights illuminated, then sat down on a chopping block by the wood pile. It was a nice little piece of property, at least what she could see at night. Lights from the valley twinkled through the trees. There'd be a great view of the valley in daylight. They might be able to see the Pacific Ocean from the loft bedrooms on the other side of the house. Matt must have put a lot of work into getting the house ready. She had the sinking feeling Jackie wouldn't go for it.

Matt was more into the relationship than Jackie was. Now, he was going to get hurt, depending on how badly Jackie reacted to all this. Relationships sucked like that, she thought. One person was always more into it than the other and then someone's feelings got stomped on.

Jackie came rushing out of the house as if a lion were at

her heels. A much more sedate Matt followed, his slumped shoulders giving Tori all the answer she'd get tonight about how their private talk went. Relationships really did suck.

Chapter 11

TORI HELD HER rain-soaked mountain bike and eyed up the damaged electric fence around the round pen. From the tangled mess, she guessed one of the horses had made a mess of it. She rolled her bike under a tree and returned to the pen.

Ashley ran up beside her. "Hey, I was about to fix this mess."

"Tank Girl giving you problems or do you just like the feel of electric zaps?"

"I can think of a few better sensations against my skin."

Tori bent down to hide her blush. "Baby horses are a pain in the ass." She tugged the band of white electric tape pulled loose from the round pen fencing. "Shouldn't be too hard to fix."

Ashley walked over to the car battery that powered the electric fencing. "You want me to unhook this before you repair the loop, or do you enjoy a good jolt now and then, too?"

Tori glanced up at her, grinning sheepishly. "Oh, yeah. That would help."

Ashley disconnected the battery. Tori wove the tape band through the plastic clips that held it to the pen fencing. Ashley reconnected the battery. After a moment, Tori heard the slow click-click from the battery that said the juice was on.

She put a finger on the upper tape and a few seconds later, grabbed it back with a jump. "It's live."

Ashley wiped the rain out of her eyes and just looked at her. "You couldn't tell that from the clicking noises? Maybe you do like it rough."

"Maybe I do." Tori picked up her bike and started walking to the hay barn.

Ashley trotted after her. "Need any help with the night feeding?"

Tori paused by the tractor, still holding her bike. "Um, are you sure you want to hang around? This rain isn't stopping anytime soon."

"It's better than packing. I'm moving back in with my grandfather."

That didn't sound good. "Is he getting worse?"

"The chemo's hitting him pretty hard. I just want to be there for him, you know? Besides, if you can handle the rain, I can handle it."

Ashley had a knack for turning the conversation away from her grandfather. Tori debated how far to push her. She remembered not wanting to talk about Keisha, either.

"All right, but you have to wear this." Tori pulled a crumpled Oakland A's baseball cap out of her backpack and handed it to Ashley. "It'll keep the rain out of your eyes anyway."

Ashley put the cap on. "What about you?"

Tori pointed to her curls. "This is water-resistant. The only perk I get from my hair."

Ashley reached out and played with Tori's curls. "I wouldn't say it's the only perk. I like your hair, it suits you."

"I'd rather have straight hair like yours." Tori tucked a few loose strands of Ashley's hair under the baseball cap. She stared into intense brown eyes and felt a rush of desire that scared her. They hadn't progressed beyond steamy kisses, but when she was this close to Ashley, she felt the burning need for so much more.

She took an unsteady step back. "Should we pack up the tractor before we get totally drenched?"

Tori stepped in the hay barn and tossed bales out to Ashley who packed the tractor wagon as best she could. Even with two of them working together, it took close to a half hour before they finished feeding all the horses. Tori's boots sank into the mud by the time they walked back to the parking lot and her bike. Her jacket was waterproof, but the rest of her was soaked and cold. Still, she wasn't ready to say good-bye, and the way Ashley hung around suggested she wasn't either.

"Let me give you a lift back home," Ashley said.

Tori wiped the rain off her face. "It's way out of your way."

Ashley took Tori's bike helmet and opened the tailgate to her truck. "Come on. You don't want to pedal uphill in this weather. Look at the hilltops. It's coming down as snow up there."

Tori looked up at the layer of white capping the Santa Cruz Mountains. "You just want to take the tourist route to visit an inch of snow."

Ashley shrugged. "So humor me."

Tori hefted her bike into the back of the truck and got into the passenger side. Ashley drove out of the stables, heading in the general direction of Tori's house. She supplied the necessary directions along the way. The drive should have taken only fifteen minutes or so, but traffic was backed up already due to both the rain and the people in the valley clogging the roads to visit snow. Her road wound up beyond most of the traffic areas and it was a clear drive after that. When they pulled into her driveway, a blanket of white covered everything, from the back patio to the clumps of her mother's garden plants that lined the parking area. No other cars were present. Tori hopped out of the truck.

Ashley got out as well and walked around the edge of the driveway. "It's beautiful up here."

"It gets like this once or twice a winter." She kicked at the snow. It couldn't be more than an inch or two. "Thanks for driving me up here."

"You already looked like a pathetic drown rat, what else could I do?"

"And you think you look any better?" Tori flicked back damp strands of Ashley's hair. "There's something I didn't tell you, about why I ditched my car."

Ashley took a step closer and put her hand on Tori's arm. "I wondered about that part, but you're not a predictable girl. That's one of the reasons I like you."

Tori shook but it was from the cold. She held Ashley's gaze

for a long time. She'd kept her drinking binge a secret. It exposed just how stupid she was.

She took a deep breath and let it out. "I was drunk. If I stayed, I'd have lost my license and who knows what else."

"Oh. That would have been bad."

Tori looked at the snowy driveway. "I haven't told that part to anyone else."

"Are you an alcoholic?"

That was an unexpected question. "No."

"That's exactly what an alcoholic would say." Ashley looked away. "My mother is an alcoholic. I don't know if I can handle it if you are, too."

Tori let out a long sigh. "I looked into it after the accident, okay? I don't have any of the symptoms of alcoholism except for drinking alone sometimes. I haven't had a drink since the accident and I don't want one. I know it was stupid to drink and drive. I'm just glad nothing worse happened."

Ashley closed the distance between them and pulled Tori into her arms. "I'm glad you told me," she whispered in Tori's ear.

Tori wrapped her arms around Ashley's waist. Snowflakes drifted down around them. She closed her eyes, enjoying the warmth of Ashley pressed against her.

Ashley slid her hands down Tori's arms until they held hands.

Tori gave her a crooked smile. "You've got seriously cold hands."

"It's seriously cold out." Ashley squeezed her hands before letting go. "The snow is sticking in your hair. Another twenty minutes and you can be a walking snowman."

Tori shook her head and sprayed Ashley with clumps of snow from her hair.

"No fair!" Ashley scooped up a small pile of snow and scrunched it into a snowball. She lobbed it at Tori's chest.

Tori bent to make her own snowball, but Ashley took off, heading around the patio into the snowy back yard. She was on

Ashley's heels in an instant. She nailed her with a snowball in the middle of her back.

Ashley slowed down. "Okay, we're even now."

"I don't think so." She tackled Ashley and took her down into a lump of white that turned out to be a snow-covered pile of leaves.

Ashley tried to roll away, but Tori pinned her down. She felt the warmth of Ashley's body beneath her. Ashley pressed Tori's back and shifted until their legs entwined. Brown eyes studied her. A tongue flicked across red lips. Tori lowered her head and closed her eyes just as those lips brushed against hers. Parting her lips, she felt that tongue teasing her. All sense of cold disappeared.

The sound of a car approaching shattered the moment.

"Shit." She rolled off Ashley and jumped up. "Come on, get up." She frantically brushed the snow of herself and Ashley, who stood in a daze. "Sorry, it's my mother."

They walked to the driveway as her mother's SUV pulled into a parking spot next to Ashley's truck. Her mother emerged from the SUV, dressed in a crisp gray business suit and carrying a laptop case slung over one shoulder and her cell phone pressed to her ear. She gave Ashley's truck the once-over before she caught sight of Tori and Ashley approaching.

Her mother flicked off her phone. "There you are. I've been trying to reach you for the last half hour, but I see you got a ride home already."

Tori waved her hand in the direction of Ashley. "Um, yeah. This is Ashley. She stables her horse at the same barn as Saxon."

Her mother pocketed her cell phone and held out her hand. "Nice to meet you. I'm Celeste, Tori's mother."

Ashley shook the offered hand.

Her mother paused only long enough to shift the shoulder strap of her bag before walking up to the back porch. "You're welcome to come inside and dry off, Ashley. You both look like you could use it."

The words spilled out of Tori's mouth before she could think. "Ashley needs to head home already."

Ashley turned to her with a puzzled expression, but didn't contradict her. She'd make it up to her, later, when she stopped panicking. Her mother couldn't have seen them making out in the snow, but it was a damned close call.

Her mother stepped inside, leaving them alone.

"I'm really sorry," Tori said. "She can't see us, you know, together."

Ashley stuffed her hands in her jacket pockets. "I guess I understand."

Ashley's expression said she didn't really understand, but there wasn't anything Tori could do about it right now. She pulled her bike and helmet out of Ashley's truck.

"Thanks again for the ride. I'll call you, later."

"Sure." Ashley turned her back to Tori and got in her truck. She didn't look back once.

Tori backed up the steps to the porch and watched until Ashley's truck disappeared down the hill. That didn't go down well. Her mother was thankfully oblivious, but Ashley was pissed off.

Life sucked sometimes.

TORI HOPPED INTO the passenger side of Matt's car. "Thanks again for the ride. I hope it hasn't been too much of a pain."

"Not a problem. Two and a half days of shuttle-service isn't that big a deal." He pulled out of her driveway and back onto the road. "I'm only five miles further up the hill now anyway."

"I'd have never been able to do this temp barn manager job for Michelle if it weren't for you. I can get my car back after she pays me for this."

"And my last useful purpose in life disappears."

Matt kept his eyes on the road, but she heard the sadness mingled with his sarcasm. "Are things that bad with Jackie?"

He shrugged. "Nothing's really different, I guess. I'm just seeing her in a different light now."

"Not a warm, fuzzy feeling, is it?" She didn't like to bad mouth someone else, but Jackie was screwing up with Matt, big time. Jackie wasn't ready for the commitment of moving in with Matt, but she could just talk about her feelings instead of the hot and cold treatment she'd been giving him lately.

And her. Jackie avoided her in everything but the history class they were all in.

She scrunched down in her seat. At least Ashley still talked to her after she explained why she shoved her away when her mother showed up. That was an easy explanation. Her mother would toss her on the street if she found out she was gay.

"Hey, you still with me there?" Matt shot her a look before focusing on the curving road again.

"Yeah, sorry, just thinking about stuff."

"What stuff?" When she didn't reply right away, he pushed on. "Come on, I've been whining at you for three days now. I'm due for some payback of the soulful heart-to-heart kind."

She caught his eye for a moment before turning away. She hadn't told anybody what she was feeling, except Jackie, and now Jackie was barely talking to her. If she talked about it with Matt, she'd have to figure it out instead of letting it linger in limbo. If she didn't talk about it though, she was going to pop. "I was thinking about a girl."

"A new girl?"

"Sort of. She stables her horse at my barn."

"How long have you known her?"

"Um, since Halloween."

Matt shot her a quick glance. "Are you serious? You've been seeing someone for months and this is the first time you tell me about it? I think I'm offended."

"It's not like that, we're not really dating."

"So what have you been doing for six months?"

"I wish I knew." She stared at the cars surrounding them on the highway. "I don't think she's my type anyway."

Matt laughed. "You don't have a type. You dated all of one person so far in your life, unless you're holding out on me."

"And this girl has dated like a hundred people, boys and girls."

"Is that why you won't date her, because she's bi?"

She tried to make sense of her tangled thoughts. "No, I don't think so. I just don't share well."

"You don't like the competition."

"No, I don't." It was more than that though. She hated feeling like she wasn't good enough for someone else, that they needed more than she could offer. Robyn treated her that way. Her mother treated her that way. Tori the disappointment, Tori who was not as good as Keisha and never could be.

She pulled back on her downward spiraling mood. That way led to a certain pocket knife she wasn't even in possession of at the moment, because of Ashley. She owed her for helping her break the cutting cycle.

Matt pulled off the highway, and they were at the barn within minutes. Tori spotted Ashley's truck as Matt came to a stop. Ashley was leading Tank Girl to the round pen, but she wasn't alone. She had Carmen with her again.

Tori paused with her hand on the door lock. Her resolve to talk things out with Ashley faded. She couldn't talk with her friend Carmen present. An ugly feeling crept up from the base of her spine, and she recognized it as raw jealousy.

"Something wrong?" Matt asked.

She pointed. "That's the girl I was telling you about, leading the horse."

Matt glanced past her. "The chubby one?"

She shot him a look.

"Um, yeah. She's kind of cute. Who's that with her?"

She looked back. "Her roommate."

Matt put a hand on her shoulder and gave her a nudge. "You can beat her. Just look at her. She hates every second of being at the barn. She's as bad as Jackie."

She watched Carmen for a moment and had to agree, she

was a fish out of water here. This was Tori's place. It was her
last day as acting barn manager, and that at least she was good
at.

Matt waved as he drove off down the muddy trail. Ashley
was making Tank Girl trot in circles at the end of a long lead
rope. Carmen was perched on the edge of a weathered bench,
looking stiff and awkward. This was Tori's element, and she
was about to prove it. She walked to the round pen and hopped
up to sit straddling the fence. Ashley saw her as Tank Girl
circled in her direction. She thought Ashley paused, but Tank
Girl didn't stop, and neither did Ashley.

Her stomach did a flip flop. Ashley didn't acknowledge her
at all. Was she being ignored because of Carmen, or some other
reason? Tori wanted to slink away, but there was no way to do
that without looking like an idiot. She took another approach
instead.

Tori knew the answer to her question but asked it anyway.
"Have you ridden her yet?"

"Michelle's the only one who can ride her." Ashley
continued leading her horse in a circle.

"I could ride her."

That made Ashley stop her slow circle and glare at her.
"Bullshit."

Tori hopped off the fence. Tank Girl continued in a trot for
another half circle before slowing down to a walk. She went
to the center of the pen and stood next to Ashley, waiting for
her reaction and trying to ignore the way her heartbeat was
pounding in her ears.

Ashley's shoulders relaxed a little. "She doesn't even have
a saddle on."

"So? I ride bareback all the time." She walked to Tank Girl
and scratched the horse's withers. She held out her hand to
Ashley, not sure if she'd get the lead rope or another rejection.

Ashley took a step closer. "Why are you doing this?" The
look in her eyes seemed to soften for an instant.

"Because I can."

"And I can't." Ashley slapped the lead rope in her outstretched hand and stalked out of the round pen.

She watched Ashley sit stiff-backed by Carmen on the bench and knew she screwed up again, like she always did. She turned back to Tank Girl. She could do this part right, at least. She led the horse to the mounting block, then looped the lead rope through the halter to form makeshift reins. Once up on the block, she leaned her weight across Tank Girl's back, like she'd seen Michelle do. The horse shifted back, but otherwise didn't react. Taking that as a good sign, she threw her leg over Tank Girl and sat bareback on her. The horse took a half-step forward, holding her head high and tense.

"It's okay." She patted Tank Girl's neck. "You can do this without a saddle."

Tank Girl lowered her head a little but remained tense. Tori tapped her sides, and the horse jolted into a quick trot before settling down to a fast walk. They walked the round pen circle twice. Ashley leaned forward as they passed her, looking a lot less angry than she had earlier. Tori tapped Tank Girl's sides again until they were trotting. The horse had a bouncing trot, more jolting than Saxon, but she kept it up for a full circle.

Finally, she was doing something right. She might be a screw-up in other areas, but she could ride. She tapped Tank Girl's sides faster, wanting to feel the rhythm of the horse in canter. Tank Girl trotted faster. She kicked harder, and the horse moved into a steady canter, something even Michelle hadn't done yet on this horse. Ashley stood up as they circled by her. Tori let go of the reins with one hand to wave as they passed.

The steady rhythm beneath her disappeared. Tank Girl bucked and turned at the same time. She held the reins with one hand and struggled to regain control, but she was unbalanced and losing her seat. She grabbed Tank Girl's mane in her free hand and tried to pull herself back up. Tank Girl gave another jarring buck, and Tori flew off backward. The ground came at her with a vengeance, and she slammed into the dirt in a twisted mess.

"Tori!" Ashley was over the round pen fence in an instant.

Gritty sand pressed into Tori's cheek. She felt pins and needles everywhere. She tried roll over. A pain so fierce laced up her spine that she bit down on her lip to keep from screaming. Her eyes stung with tears she couldn't hold back.

Ashley fell on her knees beside her. "Damn it. Why didn't you wear a helmet?"

Tears rolled off her face and dampened the sand beneath her cheek. "I can't move. My back. It hurts."

Ashley fumbled in her pockets as tears formed in her eyes. She turned back to Carmen. "Call 9-11. She needs an ambulance!"

Tori had forgotten about Carmen. She had to get her face out of the dirt. Gritting her teeth, she pulled her hand out from under her and dug into the dirt. The pain was unmerciful.

"Stay still!" Ashely covered Tori's hand.

She took an angry swipe at her tears. "Why can't I get up?"

"Help is on the way."

Her whole body shook. Ashley pulled off her coat and draped it across her back. *Wasn't that what you were supposed to do if someone was going into shock?* She wasn't that bad, what she?

She couldn't stop shaking, even with the coat on her. "I'm an idiot."

"Shut up."

Ashley stretched out on the ground next to her so they were at eye level and gingerly draped an arm across Tori's shoulder. Ashley's body heat helped, but she still trembled. Where the hell was that ambulance?

It was an agonizing age later when she finally heard the distant sound of a siren. Ashley leaned up on one elbow. Tori clutched her hand. She didn't want to be left alone.

"Carmen," Ashley said. "Run down to the road and direct the ambulance here." Carmen hurried off as fast as her fancy boots would let her. The sirens got louder and then stopped abruptly. Ashley turned back to her. "The ambulance is here. You're going to be okay."

She still held Ashley's hand in a vice grip. "Don't leave me."

Ashley leaned back down. "I'm not going anywhere."

The paramedics showed up a long minute later, a stout man and a taller woman. Ashley explained what happened, talking so fast Tori didn't know if they understood half of what Ashley said.

The female paramedic leaned next to Tori. "I bet you've had better days, eh?"

Tori gave her a weak smile. "Yeah."

"Okay, we're going to ask you some silly questions, but bear with us."

The questions led to requests for small movements, first her hands, then her toes. It ended with what she was dreading most, the move to a backboard. Ashley let go of her hand but stayed in her line of vision the whole time, right up until they put her in the back of the ambulance.

"I'll be right behind you," Ashley said as the ambulance doors shut.

TORI COULD MOVE her legs again, now that the nurse had given her pain medication and a muscle relaxant. She could even partially sit up, but it didn't improve her mood much. She'd gotten over the initial panic when the paramedics explained that she'd likely sprained her back when she twisted and fell, and that she was suffering from back spasms. What they hadn't explained was that the hospital would insist on contacting her parents. She was expecting her mother to come hollering through the hospital corridor at any moment.

The emergency room was packed, as were all the curtained-off beds for patients. She lucked out to be in an exam room with a door, even though they didn't close it. The nurses were discussing a patient who was volunteering to be admitted to a drug rehab program. She would have laughed about the lack of privacy if she wasn't sure her own medical history was being as openly discussed out there.

She heard new arguing in the hallway. It had to be her mother bitching her way to the room. Why couldn't the drugs have made her unconscious? That would make meeting her mother in a hospital room again more bearable. When the nurse came in the room, she slammed her eyes shut. Maybe she could bluff her way out of a confrontation.

She heard the nurse stop at her bedside. "Well, she's asleep so she can't confirm that you're her sister, and you have no ID so I'll need to ask you to stay in the waiting room."

Sister? She opened her eyes to see Ashley standing beside the nurse and looking frazzled and angry. It took her a moment to correlate the words Ashley and sister in the same sentence and how Ashley had bluffed her way into the emergency room. "Yes, she's my sister."

Ashley crossed her arms. "Satisfied?"

The nurse looked at her as if she didn't quite believe the two of them were related, but shrugged and left the room. Ashley closed the door, then came back to sit on the edge of Tori's bed. She looked a mess, with dust all over her clothes from the round pen and dirt smeared across her face. Tori was so relieved to see her that she had to stifle a giggle. "My sister?"

"They wouldn't let me in." Ashley picked up her hand and wrapped it in the warm cocoon of her own hands. "How are you feeling?"

She couldn't stop the heat rising in her cheeks. "Better. It's just a bad back sprain and some head lumps, but not even a concussion."

Ashley's relieved expression turned to anger in a flash. "Don't you ever do that to me again!"

Even without the pain meds, she didn't think Ashley was making any sense. "Do what?"

"Play the show-off dyke card with no helmet and an untrained horse and nearly get yourself trampled as well as broken. Did you know Tank Girl almost kicked you in the head when you fell? You'd be a whole lot worse if she had."

"Oh. Sorry." She couldn't remember the fall, but she did recall the show off bit and Ashley's girlfriend. "Sorry if I ruined your date."

"What?"

"Carmen. She's not out in the waiting room, is she?"

"Carmen?" Ashley laughed. "No, she got a ride from the barn." Her expression shifted to something unreadable. "It wasn't a date, either, and she's never really been one of my girlfriends."

She heard the hesitation in Ashley's voice but didn't push it. Not a date was a good thing, except it meant she'd acted like a jackass for nothing.

"What's wrong?" Ashley asked. "Even with your eyes going half-cross-eyed, you look like someone just kicked you in the gut. Does something else hurt?"

"Sometimes I get tired of being the perpetual screw-up, you know?"

"Why'd you get on Tank Girl? You've never tried to ride her before."

Tori stared at the ceiling tiles. "I wanted to prove I was good at something, but even that didn't work."

"You're a great rider, but hopping on the back of an untrained horse was just plain stupid. You know that."

"Yeah, well, when I saw you with Carmen, smart thinking wasn't on the menu anymore."

Ashley cupped her cheek and turned her face until they were eye to eye again. "Is that what this is about, that I used to see other people?"

Used to? She looked into Ashley's eyes and wished for all the world that she hadn't just confessed her own insecurities. She opened her mouth, ready to backpedal out of that confession when the door opened and her mother stormed into the room. She moved so fast to pull out of Ashley's hands that she sent a spasm of pain up her spine.

Her mother glared at Ashley's back. "Why are you here?"

Ashley's gaze hadn't left hers. "I'm her sister."

"Her sister is dead, not some overweight white chick."

"Mom!"

Ashley jumped off the edge of the bed and swung around to face Tori's mother. "Oh, I'm sorry. I didn't, I mean, they wouldn't let me in."

"She's my friend, Mom."

Her mother looked down at Tori but her expression didn't change. "She wasn't a good enough friend to keep you from doing something stupid again."

Tori locked her jaw shut. She wasn't going to have it out with her mother, not in front of Ashley. She'd sucked up enough embarrassment for one day.

Ashley seemed to have other ideas, though. "She didn't do anything stupid, she had an accident. Maybe if you paid more attention to her than your perfect dead daughter, you'd know that."

She thought her mother's eyes were going to pop right out of her head, along with the vein that was standing out on her forehead.

"Get out," her mother whispered through clenched teeth.

Ashley didn't move.

"Get out of this room before I have you arrested, and stay the hell away from my daughter!"

Ashley glanced back at Tori. She was torn between gratitude that Ashley had stood up for her and terror of what Ashley had just revealed to her mother. Without another word, Ashley left the room. Her attempt to slam the door behind her failed on the slow-moving hospital door.

Silence reigned in the room for a full minute before she couldn't stand it anymore. "Mom."

Her mother looked down at her. "We'll talk about this later. Right now, I have to find out how to get you released. Stay here and don't do anything . . ." She paused as if stepping over something unpleasant. "Just don't do anything."

Stupid was the word her mother just tiptoed around. Did she bypass it because of what Ashley said or because she didn't want to give the hospital staff anything else to gossip about? Her mother was all about keeping up appearances, no matter what.

She closed her eyes. It was easier than letting them go cross-eyed from the drugs. Today was just one big screw-up that would only get worse as more people found out. Ashley had stood up for her though. That had to mean something.

Exactly what that meant became evident three hours later when Tori woke up from her drug-induced nap. Her mother hadn't said two words to her after they released her from the hospital, other than to insist she not try to climb upstairs until her father came home to help her if she needed it. Tori had fallen asleep on the sofa and woke up as the drugs were wearing off. Her back wasn't the only thing that hurt now. She must have slammed down on her right shoulder as well, if the pain radiating from it was any indication. Her first attempt to sit up ended in an embarrassing whimper of pain.

Her mother eyed her over the magazine she was reading in the recliner. "You have another half hour before you can take your next dose of medication."

"Great." She shifted on the sofa, but nothing relieved the pain.

"You want to tell me what happened, now?"

No wasn't the answer her mother would have accepted, but Tori wasn't in the mood to elaborate on the nitty-gritty's of how she'd screwed up again. "I did something stupid, okay? Just like you thought."

"Shit." Her mother slapped the magazine down on the coffee table. "I get an emergency call and have to drag your ass home from the hospital, and that's the best explanation I get?"

"I was showing off and fell off a horse, is that better?"

"It's a start, and what the hell was that girl going on about at the hospital?"

Tori shut her eyes, not up for Olympic Parent Baiting.

She'd fall back asleep if she could, but her mother controlled the meds and that meant she was stuck in this nowhere argument for the duration. "She shouldn't have said what she said."

"But she did. Now I want to know why. I don't compare you to Keisha."

Tori barked out a short, bitter laugh. "Yeah, you do."

"When?"

"Every time I screw up. Why don't I apply myself like Keisha, why don't I have career goals like Keisha, why don't I relax my hair like Keisha. You lost your perfect, black daughter and all you have left now is me, a half-breed mongrel that can never replace her."

If her mother's expression was any indication, Tori just flew past gold medal into some new category. Wasn't platinum the next step up from gold? If it was, she'd just snagged her first platinum medal. Her mother stared at her through unblinking eyes with her mouth hanging open. In other circumstances, Tori would start a countdown until her mother popped, but today, she'd rather bypass the screaming and go straight to the silent treatment that usually followed.

"Don't you dare call yourself a half breed. I love you just the same as I love Keisha. No one degrades my daughters, not even you."

Today really wasn't her day. "Just skip it. When can I take my meds?"

"No, we will not skip it. You don't dump a load like that on me and just walk away."

"I'm not walking anywhere."

"Stow the sarcasm." Her mother edged closer, waving her finger at Tori. "Maybe I did compare you to Keisha once or twice, but I have never said she was perfect, nor have I ever said she was better because she was black and you're biracial."

"Oh come on. She always got special treatment."

"And if you thought beyond the tip of your own damned nose, you'd know why. Who was the odd one out in this family?

You? Or Keisha the half-sister, Keisha the step-daughter, Keisha the one who had to travel to visit her father."

For once, Tori didn't have a quick comeback. Keisha was so much older that she had never thought about what it was like for her growing up. By the time she'd recognized a difference between them, Keisha had been in high school. It was hard to admit, but maybe her mother was right and it was her own misgivings that made her feel isolated from her black heritage.

"Is this why you wouldn't visit Keisha during her last few weeks, because of me?"

She refused to accept that the glimmer of light in her mother's eyes might be the start of tears. Her mother never cried. "No, it wasn't you."

"Then why?"

Having a heart to heart with her mother sucked more than she thought it would. She preferred their usual caustic clashes. They required less of the deep thought and more of the snark. How could Tori wrap up months of guilt over how her petty jealousy of Keisha extended right to her grave? She couldn't. "I wasn't ready for her to die." It wasn't a complete lie. She wasn't ready. She needed more time to deal with her own stupid feelings before she could face her sister on her death bed.

Her mother's tears came for real now. "None of us were." She sat on the coffee table and took Tori's hand in hers. "None of us were."

Of all the fights they'd had, none of them had ended this way. She was too stunned to know how to react. She patted her mother's hand and tried not to be freaked out about it.

She was almost ready to deal with Keisha's death now. Too bad she was ten months too late.

Chapter 12

TORI LEFT HER car in the dirt parking lot and started the long, slow walk to Saxon's stable. Things with her mother improved after they'd talked about Keisha. That was almost worth the pain in her back. Almost. Why her parents gave her the car before she'd finished with the repair payments remained a mystery. She made the most of it, though, even if it did hurt like hell to sit still for the twenty minute drive down the hill. It had been three long days on the pain meds where she couldn't operate a can opener, never mind a car. Then another two days crawled by before her mother would let her out of the house. She hadn't mucked out her stable or any of the others she was paid to take care of. Now she was on mega doses of Advil, shuffling like an old lady, and determined to get her jobs done.

A truck rumbled up just as Tori hit the patch of trees that separated the parking lot from the main stables. The truck came to a stop, and Ashley and her grandfather got out. Ashley looked great, and her heart pumped a little faster. Iain didn't look as good. He was thinner than she remembered, and moved a lot slower. When Ashley hurried to his side to help him to the bench, Tori continued her shuffle along the path. Ashley was busy with her grandfather.

She emerged from the trees and saw Michelle stooped by the first barn repairing a broken plank. She made the effort to walk normally. It hurt like hell, but what was pain compared to ego anyway?

"Need any help?" she asked.

Michelle lowered the plank to the ground and straightened up. "You're back."

"Good as new," she lied.

"I doubt that." Michelle stripped off her work gloves and

took two steps toward her. "All I want to know is—were you drunk?"

"What? No!" Someone was approaching along the path behind Tori, but Michelle didn't stop.

"You've been drunk before, but not when you've had a responsibility at the barn."

She didn't flinch, keeping a blank face in the hopes that Michelle wouldn't catch on to how many times she had been drinking at the barn. "I wasn't drunk when the accident happened, I swear." Adding that she'd been sober since crashing her car wasn't going to help her case so she kept quiet about that.

"I don't know if I can believe you."

Ashley stepped up beside Tori. "You probably won't believe me either, but it was just an accident. Tori was fine before it happened."

Michelle glared at them both. "Whatever you say, but you're off barn duties for now. I found a replacement feeder. If you can't handle mucking out, let me know and I'll find someone for that, too."

"I can do it." Tori couldn't lose another job. She'd never pay off the car repair bill.

Michelle walked back to the fence and bent down to pick up the plank. Her silent dismissal stung. Tori walked her stiff, almost-normal walk to Saxon.

Ashley walked beside her until they were out of Michelle's hearing range. "Think she'll give you back the feeding job when you're better?"

"I don't know." She grabbed a muck rake and wheelbarrow and stepped into Saxon stable. There wasn't as much manure piled up as she'd expected. "Someone's been him mucking out."

"I did. I can keep doing it if you're not up for it yet."

"I can do this."

Ashley watched her from the stable door as she scooped up her first heavy pile of manure and tried to lift it into the wheelbarrow. Pain shot up her back and the muck rake fell from her hands as she let out a groan.

Ashley was in the stable in an instant. "What happened?"

"Nothing." She did a rigid-back squat to pick up the muck rake.

Ashley's hand covered hers on the rake. "Let me do it."

She stared into a pair of worried eyes. "If I don't do this, I lose the only job I have left."

"Just let me pile it in the wheelbarrow. You can push it to the muck heap yourself."

She was too tired to cave into her wounded pride. Ashley took the muck rake. Tori would never be able to shovel it all up anyway, not for all the horses she got paid to clean out. "I'll split the money with you."

Ashley was already shoveling Saxon's mess into the wheelbarrow. "You can use the money to take me out on a date."

Tori let out a nervous laugh, not sure whether to take Ashley seriously or not. Their dates had a way of screwing with her mind. She wasn't fit for anything physical anyway, even if Ashley was thinking along those lines, which she probably wasn't. Who'd want to date a messed-up person like her anyway?

When the wheelbarrow was full, she stepped up and lifted the handles. So far so good. She took a step forward, pushing the heavy wheelbarrow toward the stable door. Her back ached with every step, but it was nothing like the pain she felt when bending to scoop up the manure. She could do this. Each step fed the ache in her back, but she made it to the steaming pile of manure and shavings. After dumping the load, she pushed the wheelbarrow to the next stable. Ashley was already at work.

Watching Ashley do most of her work gave her too much time to think. Too many lost jobs, too many stupid injuries. Michelle gave her a weak smile as she passed by with the next load. Michelle wasn't angry with her, but she was something far worse, disappointed. Tori had hung around the barn for years, tagging along with Michelle like a kid sister. Michelle never complained and never told her to go away. Instead, she'd taught little things at first, about horses and fixing things. Lately, she'd been teaching Tori more about barn management and horse training. Tori risked losing all that because of one stupid mistake.

Her hand slipped into her back pocket, where her knife would have been. It was empty. She went back to Ashley and stepped beside her. "Where's my knife?"

Ashley pushed her hair out of her eyes. "In my tack room, why?"

"I want it back." She stood rigid as Ashley stared at her.

"Let's just finish up here, okay?"

She grabbed Ashley's arm when she started to walk away. "No. I want it now."

"Aren't you in enough pain already? What do you need the knife for?"

"It's mine."

Ashley threw down the muck rake. "Fine." She stomped off to her tack room and came back a minute later. Tori held out her hand, and Ashley slapped the small pocket knife into her palm. It felt cool and light in her hand. She looked down at it and ran a finger over the fake pearl handle. The knife wasn't hers. She'd stolen it from Keisha before she died. That's when she started carrying it around. That's when she started using it.

She closed her fist around the knife and walked away from Ashley. She heard footsteps following. It didn't matter. She had the knife back, and there was something she needed to do.

The muck heap steamed into the cold March air. She took in the smell of horse manure with each breath. The land sloped down into the woods beyond the muck heap, marking the edge of the barn property. Thorny brambles and dried thistle covered the space between her and the woods, a space she'd never be able to walk through.

There was no turning back if she crossed this line.

Ashley stepped beside her. "You don't have to do this, please."

Tori kept her eyes on the brambles and thistle, lifting the hand that held the knife. "Yes, I do."

She threw the knife as far away as she could. Pain laced down her back from the effort, and she bit back a cry and closed her eyes. She didn't even see where the knife landed. She'd never be able to find it.

Ashley's arms were around her. She buried her face in Ashley's shoulder, breathing in the horse smell and a faint hint of perfume. The pain in her back returned to its normal, constant ache. Sooner than she wanted to, she stepped out of Ashley's reach and brushed a dirty sleeve across her face.

Ashley was grinning at her like an idiot. It was infectious, and Tori smiled back. "Can we get back to mucking out?"

Ashley held her hand on the walk back to the stable they were working on. Tori's back was killing her, but she kept that to herself as she pushed wheelbarrow after wheelbarrow back to that muck heap. Each time she refused to look at the clearing beyond the heap. She wasn't going to be a screw-up anymore.

TORI STOOD IN her sports bra and boxers and stared at two sets of clothes on her bed. Set one had the dress shirt, pants, and a tie she'd have to hide from her family if she wanted to wear it. The other set was a baggy sweatshirt and jeans. Was her date with Ashley the fancy dress-up kind, or the casual kind?

Her brother banged on her closed door. "Your friend's here."

Shit. "I'll be right down." She threw on the jeans and sweatshirt and ran down the stairs. She froze when she saw her mother talking to Ashley in the kitchen.

"Sorry I'm late," she said and whisked Ashley out the back door before her mother could dig any further into their plans for the night. She had just enough time to notice a pair of tight black jeans and a cream-colored sweater before they were plunged into the darkness.

"I feel like an underdressed slob." Tori led the way to her car instead of Ashley's truck. She opened the passenger door.

"You look great." Ashley slipped past her and ducked into the car.

Tori shut the door. "Not as hot as you."

In the driver's seat with the engine started, Tori looked at Ashley again. Her gaze drifted down to where the sweater pulled tight across Ashley's chest. It was a hell of a good look for her.

"Uhem."

Her gaze shot back up to Ashley's face. "Where to?"

Ashley's face was plastered with a self-satisfied grin. "Pied Piper's in San Jose."

Caught leering and they hadn't even left the driveway. *Smooth, Tori.* She set the car in reverse and inched past Ashley's truck. "What's that place?"

"An under-21 dance club. I can't believe you haven't been there."

"I don't really dance, you know."

Ashley gave her arm a squeeze. "You'll love it."

Tori did enjoy the club when they finally made it there. They'd taken a detour to get something to eat and then a bit of procrastination because she was sure she was underdressed for a club. Ashley convinced her it would be so dark it wouldn't matter what anyone was wearing.

They were in the club for half an hour before the D.J. played the first slow song. She backed up to leave the dance floor, but Ashley grabbed her sweatshirt and pulled her close.

She stiffened. "We can't slow dance here."

"Why not?"

"It's not a gay club."

She tried to pull away but Ashley draped her arms over her shoulders.

"Nobody can tell you're a girl and so what if they do? We're not the only queers here. Look around." Ashley nodded at the two guys dancing next to them.

Tori relaxed and held Ashley around the waist. Ashley rested her head on Tori's shoulder. The music took hold. A slow, steady beat worked its magic, and she stroked Ashley's back.

The song ended too soon. Ashley lifted her head. Tori fell into Ashley's intense gaze. The altered beat of a faster song didn't penetrate their world.

"Ashley?"

Ashley froze in Tori's arms. "Oh, God. Not him."

"Who?"

"Nobody." Ashley dropped her arms from Tori's shoulders. "Let's get out of here."

When she didn't react, Ashley took her hand and led her through the crowded dance floor. A blond-haired guy stopped them before the exit, a shaky smile formed on his freckled face.

"Get out of the way," Ashley said.

His smile disappeared. "That's it? That's the only hi I get?"

Tori studied him in the dim light. He was a few inches shorter than she was, and wore a short-sleeved shirt that exposed muscular arms. He was okay looking, she guessed, if you liked guys.

Ashley glared at him. "Yes, that's it. Now go away."

His gaze darted between Ashley and Tori. "So you're going to screw him like you did me and then pretend he doesn't exist the next morning?" He turned to Tori. "Good luck, dude. I hope sluts are your style."

Tori slammed her fist into his gut. He doubled over. The crowd parted around them as if waiting for more, but Ashley dragged her out the exit and ran to the car. Nobody came out to see where they were.

Tori stood beside the car, still fuming.

"Unlock the car," Ashley said. "Let's get out of here before someone calls the police on us."

That jolted Tori out of her frozen stance. They were driving out of the parking lot within a minute, tires thumping as they hit the pavement too fast. Tori didn't know where she was going, and Ashley didn't seem to care.

She'd hit somebody. Her last fistfight had been when she was ten, and Keisha had pulled her off the other kid before there was a clear winner. No, that wasn't true. She was getting the snot kicked out of her, and Keisha had saved her ass.

Her knuckles hurt. She flexed each finger. They all worked. Nothing broken. She glanced at Ashley, who had a face of stone as she stared at the road ahead. Nothing good could be going through her mind after what that jerk said. Tori turned on the radio and found a rock station she could blast loud enough. Ashley leaned back and stared at the dark shadows whizzing by her window.

Tori's anger faded and she looked around to get her bearings. She'd been on autopilot heading for home, but home wasn't where she wanted to go, at least not yet. Ashley hadn't said a word since they got in the car. Tori drove another five miles before finding the exit she wanted. She drove along a quiet side street that led to a winding road up into the Santa Cruz Mountains. It ended outside a stone quarry. Her tires rumbled as they hit the gravel driveway, and she parked beside the locked gate.

Ashley looked around for the first time at the dark, deserted area. "I thought you were heading home."

"Not yet." She hopped out of the car and ran around to open Ashley's door. "Come on. I want to show you something."

Ashley got out and walked in a stiff stride next to her. If it weren't for the quarter moon and spillover light from the valley, they wouldn't be able to see a thing. She knew this place well enough to find the spot she was looking for in complete darkness. She found the hole in the fence that had been there for years and squeezed through. Ashley hesitated.

"Come on," she said. "You'll like this, I promise."

Ashley made her way through the hole, and Tori led her along a short path through the gravel piles. They emerged on the opposite side to an expansive view of the valley, its lights glittering in the night as far as they could see.

"It's gorgeous." Ashley took a step closer to the fence that now kept them inside the quarry and away from the precarious drop-off on the other side.

"Thought you might like it." She sat on the sandy ground, and Ashley took a seat next to her. She was very aware of where Ashley's knee touched hers. Ashley had a way of making her feel like a nervous teenager again, instead of the adult she was supposed to be. She wanted to put her arms around Ashley but she folded them across her chest instead and stared out into the lit-up valley below them. "I came here a lot, back when Keisha was sick."

"How long was she sick for?"

"Almost two years. The chemo worked at first, but she was pretty far along before they ever detected the cancer. It came back nine months later and just kept getting worse."

Ashley wrapped an arm around her back. The heat from Ashley's body blocked out the cold night air that had been blowing through Tori's sweatshirt. It felt good. Not just tingly good, but another kind of good as well.

"Who was that at the club?" she asked. Ashley dropped her arm, and Tori felt the coldness creeping in between them.

Ashley picked up a clump of sand and let it drift between the fingers of her other hand. "A guy I slept with."

"Yeah, I figured he was an ex-boyfriend."

"I don't have ex-boyfriends or ex-girlfriends, just people I've been with. He was the worst."

Tori flinched. Would she be in that category some day? She looked at Ashley and saw what might be tears building up in her eyes. Now wasn't the time to worry much about her future. "He couldn't let go?"

The last of the sand sprinkled on the ground beneath Ashley's hands. "He got me pregnant."

"Oh." *Now what?* The whole pregnancy and abortion thing

was always out of her league. She didn't know what to say next.

"You think I'm a slut, too, don't you?"

"What? No! Just because that jerk said something doesn't make it real."

"Come on. I'm eighteen and already had an abortion? I'm a slut. Like mother like daughter."

Tori brushed the sand off Ashley's hand and wrapped it in her own. "I don't think that at all. I think you're just you, and so what about the abortion? Half the girls in my high school had unprotected sex. I'm sure there are more abortions out there than you think."

Ashley lowered her head, and her hair fell forward, covering Tori's view of her face as she talked. "My mom had her first abortion at fourteen, then had me when she was sixteen. By the time she was my age, she'd abandoned me at my grandparents' house so she could go out and screw around some more. How much more like her could I get?"

Tori brushed back the strands of Ashley's hair, then leaned forward until her forehead rested on Ashley's. "You're not your mom, okay? I don't date moms."

Ashley barked out a laugh that sounded like she might have wanted to cry instead. "Is that what this is, a date?"

She grinned. "That depends. Am I a girlfriend, or just someone you want to be with?"

Soft lips brushed across hers, and she stifled a surprised gasp. Her eyes closed when she felt Ashley's tongue tickle her lips. She slipped her hand inside Ashley's jacket, feeling the soft sweater she'd wanted to touch all night. All thought of the cold night faded. She thought she'd go mad with wanting more.

When Ashley pulled away, she let out a long, unsteady breath. She had sandy patches on her sweatshirt, where Ashley had touched her, but she didn't want to brush it off yet.

"What's wrong?" she asked.

"Nothing." Ashley cupped Tori's face in her hands.

"Nothing's wrong, but it is late. If I don't get you home your mom's not going to let me take you on another date."

Tori grinned. There'd be a second date.

She drove them back to her house with one hand on the steering wheel and the other holding Ashley's hand. Her face was hot and her body tingling by the time they stopped in her driveway. She didn't dare kiss Ashley goodnight, but Ashley seemed to understand.

Ashley left her with a far better gift before she drove off—the answer to her earlier question about how Ashley viewed their time together. She hopped up the stairs to the back door with one thought singing in her mind.

She had a girlfriend.

Chapter 13

TORI HEAVED HER last pile of manure onto the muck heap and straightened up. Her back still ached from the accident, but she was taking care of her own horses now, mucking them all out three times a week. She was even feeding in the mornings and evenings to offset her boarding fees, but Michelle hadn't invited her to do any other tasks. Tori felt the sting of that rejection every time she came to the barn. If only she hadn't been so jealous, or acted like such an idiot.

She rolled the empty wheelbarrow back to the hay barn where they were kept. The barn was active on Saturdays, and all the other wheelbarrows were in use. She hadn't seen Ashley yet, but she knew she'd show up soon. Rather than stand around and wait, Tori went in search of something to do. She had at least another week of recovery before she'd be allowed to ride again, so that ruled out taking Saxon for a ride. Instead, she walked around the outlying pastures.

She found a loose horse grazing on the grass path next to the pasture. "It's no tastier out here."

She grabbed the horse's mane and led it back uphill. Michelle was in the gelding pasture, staring at Apostle. Next to her were the broken boards that allowed Tori's horse to escape.

"What happened?" Tori asked.

Michelle turned to her. "I'm not sure. I think they were fighting. Apostle has some nasty scratches on his legs."

Apostle pinned his ears back as Tori approached with the other horse. "Yeah, that's a good bet. What do you want me to do with this one?"

"How about we trade? Can you take Apostle down to the round pen so Ashley can check him out when she gets here? I don't think he needs a vet but she should judge that herself."

"Do you want me to come back and help you fix the fence?"

Michelle's steady gaze held her for a silent moment. "Is your back up to it?"

"Good as new, mostly."

"Mostly." Michelle grinned. "Okay, how about I take Apostle down and come back with a couple of planks. You stay here and keep the rest of the horses from escaping, okay?"

She saluted. "Be a human fence, got it."

Glad to be of use again, she waited in front of the broken fence until Michelle returned with the supplies. It only took a few minutes to fix, but it was the first time they'd worked together in weeks. When they were done, they walked back down to the main barn area, talking almost like they used to. It wasn't until they were back at the round pen where Apostle waited that Tori saw Ashley's truck, but it wasn't parked, and Ashley wasn't driving it, she was standing outside the driver's door, talking to Carmen.

Tori's smile faded. Carmen was now driving away in Ashley's truck. Ashley had admitted to sleeping with Carmen in the past. Seeing them together just had a way of feeding her jealousy monster.

"Did you overdo it with your back?" Michelle asked. "You look kind of funny."

"No, I'm fine." She turned away from Ashley who was waving at her with a broad smile. "I need to go to the toilet." She walked the long way around the pen, hoping to avoid Ashley, but it didn't help.

Ashley met her at the other side. "Hey, didn't you see me?"

"Yeah, but I need the toilet." She didn't stop until Ashley pulled her to a stop.

"Okay, what's up."

She stared at her boots. "Nothing. You should check out Apostle. He's been fighting."

"Really?" Ashley looked back at the round pen. "Wait a minute, no changing the subject. What did I do wrong?"

"Nothing."

Ashley lifted Tori's face to catch her eye. "That's not a convincing nothing."

Ashley's quirky smile melted some of Tori's anger. "It's nothing, really. I'm just being stupid."

"Stupid about what?"

Tori pointed down the road. "About your roommate."

"Carmen?" Ashley laughed. "You don't need to worry about her." She slipped her hand into Tori's. "Honest. She's my best friend, like Jackie's your best friend."

She didn't bother to point out that she'd never slept with Jackie. "I'm not sure Jackie's my best friend anymore."

"How come?"

"I took her boyfriend's side of an argument. I think she's kind of ticked. Plus, I don't drink anymore so she's bored with me."

"Sorry."

She shrugged. "Why did Carmen take your truck?"

"She's helping her cousins move some furniture."

"She's helping?" Tori couldn't hide the sarcasm in her voice. She couldn't picture Carmen with her perfect hair and perfect clothes lifting some sofa into a truck bed.

Ashley laughed. "Yeah, you're right. She's just driving my truck. The rest is up to her cousins." She stepped closer. "Can we go to Saxon's stable?"

"What for?"

"You know. . ." Ashley blushed.

"You mean for this?" Tori closed the gap between them and kissed Ashley on the lips, hearing her gasp in surprise. She nibbled her lip before stepping back with a grin. "Everyone here knows I'm queer. They all knew my ex-girlfriend."

"Humph." Ashley frowned. "And I'm supposed to be happy about that?"

Tori kissed her on the cheek. "You can be happy about this, right?"

"Yes, I can. And you can be happy, too, because I told my grandfather."

Tori froze. "You came out to your grandfather?"

Ashley gave her a puzzled look. "Yeah, is that a problem?"

"No, it's none of my business." She extricated herself and started down the path to the portable toilet again.

Ashley caught up and stopped her. "Okay, now what did I do wrong?"

"I won't come out to my parents for you." Tori jammed her fists into her pockets. It was like a bad replay of her breakup with Robyn. She waited for the inevitable anger and shouting that had happened the last time, but it didn't come. She looked at Ashley and saw the sadness she was causing. That was worse than the hollering. "Sorry. I just can't."

"I never asked you to."

"But you will. And then it'll all fall apart again."

Ashley's expression darkened. "I'm not your ex-girlfriend if that's what this is all about. I told my grandfather because I wanted him to be happy for me, and because this is the first time since junior high that I've even tried to date someone for more than a weekend."

"Sorry." Tori stared at her boots again, kicking at the mud with her heel.

"Don't be." Ashley let out a sigh. "Seriously. I'm happy, he's happy, and I won't ever pressure you into telling your parents."

Tori dug her fingernails into her palms. "My dad would be okay I think. My mother comes from the praise-Jesus camp."

"They don't sound too gay-friendly, do they?"

"My guess is no."

Ashley tugged at Tori's jacket sleeve until Tori took one hand out of her pocket. Ashley wrapped her hand around Tori's. "I knew my grandfather would be okay with it. If I had a mother like yours, I probably wouldn't tell her either. I've known people who were kicked out of their house when they came out. I wouldn't want you to go through that."

She squeezed Ashley's hand. "Thanks. Um, I need to hit

the portapotty, though, for real. I'll meet you back at the round pen?"

"Apostle, I forgot. Are we okay here?"

Tori gave her a crooked smile. "Yeah, we're okay. Thanks."

Ashley leaned in and kissed her. "Who knew you were such a high-maintenance dyke?"

"Right." She ran off to take care of business, happy that things hadn't gone horribly wrong, like they had with Robyn.

TORI SCOWLED AT her bedroom. No level of cleaning could make it right, not for tonight. She looked at her clock. She'd been cleaning since her family had left, almost two hours ago. She had another forty-five minutes until Ashley showed up.

The bed sheets were all wrong. She couldn't have Ashley spend the night on old sheets. She yanked them off, rolled them in a ball, and stuffed them in her closet. There was only one place where she could get new sheets.

Keisha's room.

She opened Keisha's bedroom door. Keisha's original bed was back in there. The flowery comforter was a bust, but Tori had put the new sheets on the bed herself. She peeled off the comforter and folded it on the edge of the bed. Brand new light blue sheets stared back at her. Perfect.

Ten minutes after she finished her last-ditch effort on her bedroom, she heard a truck drive up. She ran downstairs and stood in the kitchen doorway until Ashley climbed the patio steps.

Ashley looked great. So great, Tori had to stop a stream of mental images that would make her blush soon.

Seeing Ashley looking so relaxed made her wonder what exactly they would get up to tonight. Maybe Ashley thought it was going to be movies and popcorn all night. Maybe Tori would be taking a cold shower to keep from combusting if they didn't connect tonight.

"What's the funny look for?" Ashley asked.

"Nothing." Tori stepped aside to let Ashley enter.

Ashley held out a duffle bag. "Where should I put my stuff?"

"In the living room is fine." She led the way through the kitchen. It also bore the stamp of her cleaning fit, but not as much, since her mother made sure everyone put their own dishes away.

"You wouldn't believe the lecture my grandfather gave me. All about the birds and the bees and when's the right time for 'physical intimacy' as he put it."

Tori looked down at her socks, a little smile tugging at the corner of her lips. "Oh." So maybe Ashley didn't think it was going to be an uneventful night.

Ashley dumped her bag in the living room and plopped on the sofa. "Anything as good from your parents before they left?"

"More like no drinking and smoking and if anything is broken when they come back, I'll be paying for repairs."

"Hah. So I guess those doobies in my bag will go unlit."

Tori's eyes widened. "You didn't bring weed, did you?"

"No, I didn't. Can't stand the stuff."

"So what is in the bag?"

Ashley blushed. "Just pajamas and stuff."

Tori couldn't imagine what was blush-worthy about pajamas so it had to be the stuff that turned Ashley's cheeks red. Hers were following suit.

Ashley patted the sofa next to her. "What's the plan for tonight?"

She took a seat next to Ashley and felt a lot more nervous all of a sudden. "Um, not much. I thought maybe we'd watch some videos. I can make popcorn if you want." Talk about falling back on the Chicken's Guide to Dating.

"I came prepared." Ashley hopped off the sofa and dug in her bag. Tori peered over but didn't see any of the infamous stuff.

Ashley pulled out a handful of videos. "Are you in the

mood for sweet lesbian romance, hot lesbian romance, or funny lesbian romance?" She handed Tori the three videos.

"Wow, where'd you get these?" Tori flipped each DVD case over to read the back.

"Mail order. They come in nice little packages with no description on them."

Tori wondered what else in that bag came in nondescript packages. She handed Ashley the hot lesbian romance to watch first, just to prove she was ready for whatever Ashley had in mind.

She ran into the kitchen to make the popcorn while Ashley squatted down to figure out the entertainment system. It would be an interesting night for sure.

TORI'S EYES WERE burning in their sockets with the first movie. She didn't actually regret picking it, but she didn't know what to do with her nervous energy by the time the credits were rolling across the TV. Ashley sat next to her on the sofa, munching the remains of the popcorn and not looking at her at all. Was she just as nervous or was she just waiting for Tori to give her a sign and they'd be stripped and reenacting the movie before Tori knew what hit her?

Tori hopped off the sofa. "I bought frozen pizza. Are you hungry?"

Ashley eyed the empty popcorn bowl. "I guess."

It wasn't an emphatic yes, but it wasn't a no either, and Tori needed a little physical distance to recover from that last steamy scene. She sped to the kitchen and banged through the cupboards looking for the right tray to stick the pizza on. The directions said stick it right on the oven rack but if she got so much as one drop of sauce in the oven, her mother would make her scrub the whole thing out on Monday.

She had the pizza on bake when Ashley joined her in the kitchen. Tori watched her out of the corner of her eye while she set the oven timer. Ashley was quiet, unusually quiet. That piqued her curiosity. "Did you like the movie?"

Ashley glanced up at her with a grin. "Oh yeah. It's one of my favorites. How about you?"

"I don't know. Some parts weren't really realistic, you know?"

"The plot wasn't really why I like the movie."

"Oh." She picked up a spoon from the counter and twirled it to give her hands something to do. When Ashley took a step toward her, the spoon slipped through her fingers and clattered onto the kitchen floor. "What movie do you want to watch next?"

"How about we play poker until the pizza's ready?"

She laughed. "Strip poker, I bet."

"You said it." Ashley stared at her as if daring her to back down. She just shrugged and went to find a deck of cards. She was pretty good at poker and really, how much trouble could they get into in the twenty minutes it took for the pizza to cook?

Thirty-five minutes later, the oven was off and the pizza ignored. She sat in only her t-shirt and boxers. Ashley sat in even less. She went from staring at her cards to peeking at Ashley. Distracting wasn't the word that came to mind, more like maddening. She didn't want to be playing cards anymore. She wasn't interested in the pizza drying to a crisp in the oven either. The oven had turned off when the timer went off, so the pizza could wait. She didn't think she could much longer.

"Are you going to play your hand?" Ashley asked.

The cool air was having an effect on Ashley, that was obvious, but Tori wasn't going to mention it if Ashley didn't. She played her hand, weak though it was.

"Hah! My pair of eights beats your king high. Take it off, Tori."

Ashley's triumphant grin nipped at her pride. She folded her arms across her soon-to-be bare chest. "We should eat the pizza before it gets all dried out."

"Oh no you don't. I've been freezing my nibs off here for the last few minutes. If you don't take something off, I'll take it off for you."

"I'd like to see you try."

She kept an eye on Ashley as she walked to her. Ashley walked behind her chair, and she tensed, waiting for an attack to strip off her t-shirt. Instead, warm hands rested on her shoulders, fingers playing with the her shirt but not trying anything, yet. Ashley slid her hands down Tori's crossed arms, and Tori went from feeling warm to hot in a flash. She felt the heat of Ashley's body on her back.

It took an age and yet no time at all to stand and face Ashley. One heated kiss, and she was leading Ashley back to the sofa, back to where the memory of that movie still ignited ideas in her head. Maybe it was the right movie to choose first, she thought as Ashley wrapped herself around her, and they sank into the plush cushions.

Ashley's first kiss was hard and insistent, her tongue demanding entry. She wanted to slow things down, but Ashley was in control. She tried to shut off her brain and just enjoy the moment.

"We don't have to do anything if you're not comfortable," Ashley said.

The trouble with being brave was that it left no room for chickening out. She covered Ashley's lips with her own. If only she could shut down her own doubts as fast.

TORI WOKE UP hours later to the smell of eggs and coffee. She blinked the sleep out of her eyes and stretched. Sofa's didn't make for good sleeping. Ashley was in the kitchen, her brown hair cascaded in a tangled mess over her shoulders. Tori remembered the scent of that hair beside her last night.

Ashley paused in her breakfast preparations, turned, and gave her a broad smile. "Hey sleepy. It's almost ready."

Tori gave a half smile, nervous again. "You could have woken me up."

Ashley moved the pan off the heat, wrapped her arms over Tori's shoulders, and gave her a kiss on the forehead. "And ruin that peaceful look while you slept? That would be no way to start the morning."

"It's afternoon, you know." She got a smack on her backside for that before Ashley returned to her cooking.

"You like fried eggs I hope? I couldn't find any bacon."

"Eggs are good." She pulled out two glasses and poured orange juice. "I see you found the coffee."

"Can't live without it." Ashley slipped two eggs onto a plate for Tori and then cracked another two in the pan for herself.

Tori wolfed down her eggs. They'd never managed to eat the pizza the night before. By the time Ashley sat down with her breakfast, Tori was tearing through a bowl of cereal and contemplating re-heating that pizza. Ashley kept looking at her while she ate, but Tori wasn't sure if she was supposed to say something about the night before or just keep quiet about the whole thing.

Ashley placed her knife and fork down. "Okay, you're killing me here. Say something, would you?"

Tori gulped down the last of her orange juice. "You mean like, thanks for breakfast?"

"No, I don't mean thanks for breakfast." Ashley ran her hands through her hair until they snarled in the tangles, then she gave a long sigh. "Are you okay with what we did last night?"

Tori's cheeks were burning hot. "It was fun."

"Fun." A slight frown creased Ashley's forehead, then disappeared an instant later. "I can live with fun. Do you want to go have some more fun?"

"I can't." She pushed back from the table and rushed to the sink with her plate. "I have to get the barn. I traded morning feeding duties with Michelle in exchange for mucking out and grooming her horses."

"Oh."

She heard the disappointment in Ashley's voice but she felt too awkward to say anything more. It wasn't until after Ashley drove off that Tori relaxed enough to think about why she'd acted like a jerk. Their night together had been better than great, and that was the problem. Ashley had proven just how much more experienced she was, and how much of a novice Tori was. Now that they'd slept together, how long would Ashley stick around?

Chapter 14

TORI MADE THE turn up the road to Matt's cabin. Jackie had talked nonstop since she picked her up at college but now that they were almost at the cabin, she had become a glowering statue of silence in the passenger seat. "It's just past this hill."

"I remember." Jackie zipped up her coat in preparation. "Thanks for driving me up here. I don't know why Matt couldn't have just taken this junk up himself."

The trunk was stuffed with old plates and dishes that Jackie's mother had given Matt for his new place. Tori knew why Matt left the stuff with Jackie. He still hoped she'd come around and agree to move into the cabin with him. The way Jackie had turned to stone, Tori didn't think she'd come around, ever.

She parked the car outside the cabin and popped the trunk. Jackie went to unlock the door, and Tori followed with the first box of dishes. Matt had put a lot of work into the place since her last visit. The walls were freshly painted and the hardwood floors glowed as if he'd either scrubbed like mad, or maybe re-varnished them. Each window had a new set of curtains, the kind that looked homemade. He was the kind of guy who'd sit down and sew them himself, just to make the place look more inviting for Jackie.

It wasn't working though. Jackie ignored everything and rushed back and forth between the car and the kitchen to dump her mother's donations as fast as possible. When they were done, Tori lingered in the cabin, trying to think of a way to bring Jackie around, for Matt's sake. She walked into each room, but Jackie didn't follow.

When she stepped out of the bigger bedroom, Jackie was pulling out a flask of whiskey. "We should go outside with that."

"We?" Jackie took a long swig. "You say that as if you were going to enjoy this with me."

It was one of their main sore points right now, that she wasn't Jackie's drinking buddy anymore. Jackie continued her drink, making no move to step outside with it. Tori opened the front door. "We should probably leave before Matt gets home."

Jackie turned and blew stale alcoholic breath in her face. "If you're so worried about poor Matt's feelings, why don't you move in here with him? Boys aren't your thing, are they? How about your bi girlfriend, then? Maybe she's interested in living up in the middle of nowhere with him. Maybe he's even her type. You said you were expecting her to dump you anyway."

Tori stomped out of the house, got in her car, and started it with an excessive amount of gas. The loud rev of the engine triggered her countdown. Jackie had exactly thirty seconds to join her, or she'd drive off and leave her there. She wished she'd kept her worries about Ashley to herself. Jackie was vicious when she was in a bad mood. Tori was fed up with being the sponge that soaked up her insults.

Jackie got in the car before the thirty seconds ran out. Tori spun the car around in a circle and drove through the cloud of dust she'd kicked up to reach the dirt road. She hooked her iPod up to the stereo and cranked the music as loud as she could stand it. Jackie said nothing for the entire ride down hill. Neither did she.

TWO HOURS LATER, with the sun disappearing behind the Santa Cruz Mountains, Tori finally made it to the barn for the evening feeding. She had just enough time to say hello to Michelle and head for the hay barn before Ashley cornered her.

"We need to talk," Ashley said.

Tori hesitated outside the hay barn. She probably wasn't going to like whatever Ashley had to say. "Okay, but I have to feed before it gets too dark."

"Fine, I'll help you feed."

That decision worked in Tori's favor. The distribution of hay to each horse gave her enough excuses to avoid a serious conversation. Years of being evasive with her mother proved useful for once. By the time they rattled back to the hay barn with an empty hay tractor, she'd sidestepped every effort to talk about the night they'd spent together. She could tell Ashley was ready to scream.

When they hopped out of the tractor for the last time, Ashley fired her most serious question. "Are we still dating?"

Tori couldn't look at her. Here was the brush-off she'd been expecting all along. "Maybe you should tell me."

"What's that supposed to mean?"

With a shrug, she pulled out the tractor key and headed off to Michelle's stable where it was kept.

Ashley grabbed her by the arm. "So you slept with me and now you're ready to toss me aside, is that it?"

She pulled her arm away. "That's your motto, not mine." She stomped off to Michelle's stable, leaving Ashley behind. She dropped off the key and made it all the way to her car before Ashley ran after her.

"Wait." Ashley gasped to catch her breath.

Tori paused, keys in hand. She was not going to get off without the official "thanks and good-bye" speech. She took a deep breath and waited as Ashley walked around the car to stand next to her.

Ashley put a hand on her arm, gentler this time. "It's not like that, not this time."

"What do you mean?"

"I don't want us to be over, not like this." Was Ashley's expression softening or was just her imagination? "It's different with us, in a good way."

Tori heard the words, but didn't know how to react. "Are you sure you don't want someone with more experience?"

"I'm so sorry, I shouldn't have pushed you so far. It's just, I love being with you. I like having a girlfriend."

Girlfriend? Ashley wasn't trying to dump her after all. Chalk that up to another one of her idiot moments.

She enveloped Ashley's hand in hers. "Me, too."

Before she could lean in and steal the kiss she so desperately wanted, a pair of harsh headlights interrupted them. Tori flinched and took a step back. Chances were it wasn't her parents, but she couldn't risk it. It was the shortest kiss and make up routine on record. Unfortunately, without the kissing part yet, but she'd fix that as soon as they found out who was coming to the barn so late.

The car rumbled to a stop next to them, a shiny new Beetle that wasn't going to be as shiny after driving in the dirt parking lot. The door opened, and Jackie stepped out.

Jackie took Tori by the arm with a big smile. "Come see my new birthday present."

Tori didn't know what to say. Jackie had been avoiding her since the trip to Matt's new place. Even on a good day, Jackie hated the horse stables, but if she was making the effort to mend their friendship, Tori shouldn't ignore it. "Okay, but give me a minute here."

Jackie glanced at Ashley. "Don't take too long. I don't want my new baby exposed to this dirt much longer."

She waited until Jackie walked back to the car before she took Ashley's hand again. "Sorry for the quick exit, but I should try and mend things with her."

"We're okay, though?"

She leaned in and kissed Ashley. "More than okay."

Jackie waited for her by the car. "Well, what do you think?"

"It's nice." She was more focused on watching Ashley get in her truck than the tour of Jackie's new car.

"Remember how we celebrated my birthday last year?"

"Three bottles of champagne because you turned eighteen."

"Look inside."

She opened the passenger door and saw bottles of coke and rum in a bag.

"That's for later." Jackie started up the engine. "Let's go show this baby off."

Jackie drove around for a while, keeping up a stream of mindless chatter. Tori took a better look at the car Jackie's parents had given her. It was new all right, from the expensive GPS to the leather seats. *Must be nice to have parents with money to burn*, she thought.

Jackie pulled into the empty parking lot at their old high school. "We had good times here."

Tori gave a noncommittal grunt. Whatever good times Jackie was remembering didn't include her most of the time. Keisha's illness had swallowed up her senior year at this place. Just being back in the parking lot made her skin crawl.

"You ready for that drink?"

The rum and coke. She could almost taste it already. They'd come here more times than she could count to have a few drinks. Sometimes just the two of them, sometimes with Robyn and Matt. High school. Almost a year later, it still sucked. "I'll pass."

Jackie smiled, but a sadness had crept in. "I forgot, you're a straight arrow now."

"I wouldn't say straight."

"Things going well with the new girlfriend?"

"Ashley, yeah so far."

"That's good. I know you like that whole couple thing."

Jackie tapped her fingers on the steering wheel, the only sound in the car for a few minutes. Then she shrugged off whatever was bothering her and turned on the engine. "I should probably take you back. Don't want to be waving the demon of alcohol in front of the girl who's going clean."

The drive back was short. She was too focused on wondering what was really up to realize that Jackie had ended their reunion drive in Tori's driveway. "My car's still at the stable."

"I'll pick you up in the morning and take you back to your car." Jackie's smile was more forced now. "I'll call you tomorrow."

She got out and waited for Jackie to pull out of the driveway. Something was wrong, but Jackie obviously wasn't ready to talk about it, whatever it was. She shrugged and walked into the house. At least her own life was getting less complicated.

Chapter 15

JACKIE WAS LATE. It was a good thing Tori didn't have to feed the horses this morning or there'd be a herd of angry animals waiting for her. She'd been smart enough last night to call in someone else to feed.

She was sitting on the kitchen counter, slurping her morning Coke when her mother shuffled into the room in her slippers and bathrobe.

"You look like hell," Tori said.

"I'm catching a cold. Someone called while I was in the bath. Did you check the messages?"

"No." At the sound of a car approaching, Tori polished off her soda. "My ride's here." She hopped off the counter, leaving the soda can behind to taunt her mother. She grabbed a jacket, stuffed her feet in her untied work boots, and ran out the door. Her laces trailed behind her as she jumped down the last few stairs and hustled into Jackie's car.

"Sorry I'm late, but you know nine o'clock is still pretty early for us normal people."

That was as close to an apology as Tori would get. "It's okay. I got someone else to fill in for me at the barn this morning."

"Great! Let's go out for breakfast then. I'm starved."

"I still need to muck out."

"You want IHop? My treat."

Tori glared at her when Jackie glanced her way.

"Oh all right. Starbucks and a muffin, then. I can't face that horse stench on an empty stomach."

Twenty minutes later, after the Starbucks excursion, they drove into the parking lot at the barn. The first thing she noticed was her father's van. Michelle and Ashley were there as well, hitching up Michelle's trailer. Tori hopped out of the car and was accosted by Ashley.

"I've been calling you for the past hour." Ashley's voice had a nervous edge to it.

"Sorry. I left my phone in my car."

"Saxon is colicing again."

Ashley's words didn't register until Tori saw her father leading Saxon to Michelle's trailer. Reality slammed into her gut, and she ran to her horse. He was covered in sweat and dust. "How bad is he?"

"Bad. We're taking him to Pioneer Vet Hospital." Her father led Saxon to Michelle's trailer. Tori brushed the dirt off Saxon's face. She wanted to shout that it wasn't her fault this time, that she hadn't done anything wrong, but it didn't matter. Her horse was heading to the vet hospital for colic and that meant it could be fatal.

When they got to the trailer ramp, she took the lead rope from her father and coaxed Saxon into the trailer. There would be no feedbag to keep him occupied during the ride. She wanted to stay in the trailer with him, but it would be too dangerous. When she stepped out the trailer side door, her father was already in his van and Michelle was locking the back of the trailer up. Jackie and Ashley were where she'd left them, watching her. She locked her eyes on Ashley's and saw a reflection of her own worries in Ashley's face.

Michelle walked in front of her, breaking the spell. "Are you coming with me or your Dad?"

"With you." She took one last glance back at Ashley before running around to the passenger side of Michelle's truck and climbing in. As the truck rumbled out of the parking lot, she bit down on her lip to keep from crying. Saxon had to be okay.

SITTING IN A waiting room sucked. After an hour, Tori couldn't stand it anymore and went outside, where the rehab paddocks were. She paced around the outside of the paddocks until Michelle came out of the hospital and dragged her to a bench.

She sat, but one leg bounced up and down. "Any news?"

"Your father's still with the hospital staff. If there's any news, he'll come out and tell us. Sometimes horse's are prone to colic, and we never learn what causes it."

Tori's leg bounced faster. "What if we did know the cause, I mean for the first episode?"

"He's much worse this time." Michelle let out a short sigh. "But, if you know something, you should share that information with Saxon's vets."

Tori couldn't wait any longer. If it meant helping Saxon, she had to tell her dad the truth. She stood up and walked back to the hospital.

Her father met her at the door. "I've got good news and bad."

Good news meant Saxon would be okay, right? Who knew what passed for good news with her dad. "Bad first."

"He has a tumor that's causing the blockage. The good news is it's operable. He's going into surgery now."

Tori stuffed her hands in her pockets. "I overfed him."

Her father frowned at her. "Excuse me?"

"The last colic episode. I was mad and wasn't thinking. I rode him until he was sweaty and then threw hay at him. Then I put him in his stable with even more hay." She looked her father in the eye. "I made a stupid mistake, and I should have told you right way. I'm sorry."

"Yes, you should have told me." Her father put a hand on her shoulder. "That didn't cause this tumor, though. You couldn't have prevented this."

"Will he be all right?"

Her father led the way back into the hospital. "We'll know better after the surgery, but the procedure isn't complicated and we caught the tumor early. He'll be here for at least seventy-two hours for post-surgical care. After that, it'll be months of rehab. Are you ready for that?"

"Yes." Tori took her hands out of her pockets. "Tell me what I need to do, and I'll do it."

She'd be a grownup for once, with Saxon and with the rest of her life. No more screw-ups, and no more hiding the truth from people.

TORI KICKED MORE rocks over the edge of the gravel pit, listening to them bounce down the steep slope. The sun had disappeared behind the Santa Cruz Mountains, and she was left in a world of deepening shadows. She looked down into the pit and wondered what was at the bottom. In all the years she'd come here, she'd never thought about where the pit ended.

The quiet sounds of dusk were interrupted by footsteps. She didn't turn around. If it was the cops or the owners, they could just get through the fence and come get her. She sat down and tossed pebbles into the pit, ignoring the sound of someone working their way through the same hole in the fence she used.

The footsteps stopped behind her. "Hey."

Ashley? She turned around to stare up at a familiar face now masked in shadow. "How'd you know I was here?"

Ashley shrugged. "Just a guess. Any chance you want to sit a bit further back from the edge? I'm afraid of heights."

Tori shuffled back to the fence line. Ashley took a seat next to her and leaned against the chain link fence. Tori picked up more pebbles to give her hands something to do. "Saxon is okay."

"Yeah, your mother told me."

She rested her elbows on her knees. "It's been a crappy day."

Ashley mimicked her pose. "That we agree on."

Something in Ashley's attitude struck Tori as being off. "What's up?"

Ashley rubbed her palms into her eyes. "My grandfather's worse. He has to go for an operation. Then he's moving in with my uncle. I'm supposed to move in with them. Tori, he's treating this all like he's not going to get better."

She shifted closer and wrapped her arm around Ashley. The

next thing she knew, they were both crying, Ashley in big, hiccupping sobs, and her in quiet tears she hid behind Ashley's back as she hugged her. Why was everything getting shitty all of a sudden? Wasn't college supposed to be great, the good old times that older people reminisced about? If so, she didn't want to see what kind of crap the rest of life brought along.

Ashley settled down, taking a few long breaths. "Sorry." She pulled away, and Tori let her go.

Tori brushed away the remnants of tears before Ashley saw them. They kissed, a slow, lingering kiss. This time, there was no interruption, no car headlights to stop them, no crises to get in the way. The air was cool but Tori was getting warm. She lay down in the dirt and Ashley curled up against her. For a time, their messed-up world disappeared.

Chapter 16

TORI HELD THE cell phone in one hand while she tried to jam her notebook into her backpack, but her lunch was getting squished in the process.

"Are your grunts supposed to be turning me on?" Ashley asked over the phone. "Because it's not really working."

Her cheeks heated up. "I'm trying to repack my backpack."

"Good. I'd hate to think you were making a scene in public."

She looked at the people rushing past her. She sat in her usual place at college, the patch of grass opposite the bookstore, and as usual, she was by herself since Jackie stopped showing up. "There isn't a soul here who would notice if I was sitting here butt-naked."

Ashley's response was inaudible over the sound of someone laughing in Tori's other ear. She turned around to see Matt plop down next to her.

"I'd not only take notice, I'd take pictures." Matt flipped open his cell phone and took a picture of Tori sitting beside him. "I'm ready."

"Oh shut up," she said, giving him a whack.

"Excuse me?" Ashley said over the phone.

"Not you," Tori said. "My friend, Matt, just showed up. Say hi, Matt." She held out the phone.

"Hi," he said.

She put the phone back to her ear. "That's my friend Matt. He's okay, for a dude and all." He whacked the back of her head with a magazine but she ignored him. "We're on for tomorrow, right?"

"You don't have to do this," Ashley said.

"Yeah, I do. Girlfriends, remember? Anyway, I'll see you then."

She hung up fast to keep Ashley from hearing Matt's pathetic sing-song of "Tori's got a girlfriend."

"And you need to shut up." She whacked Matt back in the arm. "Where have you been? I haven't seen you in weeks."

He rubbed his arm, pretending it hurt. "Sorry. I wasn't sure whose side you'd take, so I stayed away."

"What are you talking about?"

"You haven't talked to Jackie lately?"

"Yeah, but she didn't say anything. What's going on?"

Matt studied his shoes for a minute before answering. "We broke up."

"Oh, sorry." That explained why Jackie popped over to the barn the other night. It wasn't just to show off her new car. It was her way of keeping Tori on her side of the breakup. "Was it because of the cabin?"

He shrugged. "I think it was more than that. I mean I wasn't forcing her to move in with me or anything, but she wasn't the same after I brought it up. She kind of disappeared for a while, and I got the hint."

Jackie didn't even have the guts to break up with him face to face. "That was pretty shitty."

He shrugged. "At least the cabin's nice. You should come up sometime. It's got the best sunrise."

"I live just down the road, remember? I see the same sunrise." Not that she was up at that hour, unless she hadn't gone to bed yet.

"Yeah, but my cabin's higher up the mountain, so I see the sun before you."

"Sure it is." She remembered the tidy two bedroom cabin and how the redwoods towered over it. Knowing Matt, he probably hacked a view through the trees just for Jackie. "You put a lot of effort into that place."

He kicked his heel into the grass, pulling up a clump. "Talk about a waste."

Tori grinned at him as an idea formed in her mind.

"What?" He looked at her with a puzzled expression.

"I wouldn't say it was a waste." Her idea solidified. Now she just needed the right pitch. She watched Matt's eyes widen as he tried to figure out what was going on in her head. Yep, all she needed was the right pitch for both of them.

TORI PULLED UP in the driveway next to Ashley's truck. She'd finally convinced Ashley not to take this trip alone. It was bad enough that Ashley's grandfather was so ill he had to move in with her uncle, but then he begged Ashley to be the one to tell her estranged mother about his cancer. That was a lot to handle solo.

She rang the door bell, and Ashley stepped out seconds later.

"Are you sure you want to come?" Ashley asked. "It's going to be frigging miserable."

"I'm sure. Besides, my car will be easier to park in San Francisco."

"South San Francisco." Ashley opened the passenger door before Tori had the chance to rush over and play the chivalry card. Ashley didn't look in the mood anyway as she plopped down on the seat and shut the door.

"Do you have the directions?" Tori asked when she sat in the driver's seat.

"101 North. I've got the rest here." Ashley patted the front pocket of her jean jacket. The paper crinkled under her hand.

Tori pulled out of the driveway without another word. Ticky tacky houses disappeared, replaced by the industrial sprawl that followed route 101 up the peninsula. She turned on the radio to fill the silence.

They drove for a half hour, then Ashley leaned forward. "See that hill up on the left? That's where my new prison will be."

Tori glanced to the side. "Your uncle's place? They're that bad?"

"Yes, that bad. No wonder my mother left when she was eighteen if they treated her the same way they treat me."

Tori hesitated a minute or two. Ashley was an emotional time bomb. Maybe it wasn't the best time to ask questions.

Ashley must have known she was building up to something. "Go ahead, ask it," she said.

The car hummed along for another minute before Tori managed to spit out what she was thinking. "Are you going to be okay, you know, with meeting your mother again?"

Ashley shrugged. "I haven't got much choice, have I?"

Tori shot her a quick look. "I could deliver the message, if you want. You don't have to see her."

Ashley stared out the side window. "Tempting offer. I haven't seen the woman in years. I don't even think of her as my mother, except when my uncles remind me of just how far this apple didn't fall from that tree. I've been living under the shadow of her mistakes my whole life."

"Then let me do it. Your grandfather just wanted her to know how sick he was, right? It won't matter if you weren't the one to tell her."

Ashley smiled for the first time. "You don't know my grandfather very well. This is his hint that I need to bond with my mother." She looked back out the window. "He has a point, you know. If he dies, I have nobody."

Tori took Ashley's hand and held it tighter than she should have. "You still have me."

"Aww, that's sweet." Ashley leaned over and kissed her on the cheek. "Sappy, but sweet. I promised my grandfather I'd do this. I couldn't face him afterward if I let you do the talking for me."

So much for that rescue attempt. "We're nearing South San Francisco."

Ashley took the directions out of her pocket and navigated them off the highway and into the city. They spent fifteen minutes twisting and turning through the city until they found the right street and then another five minutes to find parking. Ashley offered to let Tori stay behind but Tori wasn't going to desert her. They walked up to the front of the half-way house together. The building was like every other one on the block, a two-story townhouse painted light green, tucked between a beige and a light blue house that looked identical except for the colors. There was nothing on it to say it provided temporary housing for recovering alcoholics. It was just another splash of pastel in a tidy block of houses.

"Are you ready?" Tori asked.

Ashley took a deep breath and let it out. "Let's get it over with." She marched up the five steps to the front door and rang the bell.

Tori stepped up next to Ashley. A heavy-set woman with gray hair and black-framed glasses unlocked the door and peered out at them. Ashley paused. Did she know what her mother looked like?

"I'm looking for Peggy Metcalf," Ashley said.

The woman eyed her up and down. "Who are you?"

Ashley glared back at the woman. "I'm her daughter."

The woman's eyes widened just a little, and she opened the door and waved them inside. Social skills didn't seem to be a big issue for the woman as she shuffled off in her slippers without another word. Ashley couldn't seem to handle the cramped confines of the narrow hallway and walked into the nearest room, an unoccupied living room from the looks of it, though it lacked a TV. Tori followed her in and walked around the tiny room, picking up knickknacks and peeking through the lace curtains to look outside.

Ashley sat on the edge of a chair. Her heel tapped out a rapid beat as they waited. Tori wasn't convinced Ashley would last long if her mother didn't show up soon. She should have insisted on delivering the message.

Ashley jumped out of the chair as if she were ready to take off and slammed into a small, round woman with dyed black hair. The woman landed on her backside in the middle of the hallway.

Tori looked down at a pair of brown eyes identical to Ashley's. She squeezed past Ashley to help her mother up off the floor.

Heads peered out at them from three other doorways along the corridor, plus a few on the staircase leading to the second floor. Great. Ashley was the main entertainment for the day. Tori shuffled them all back into the living room to get them away from so many eyes.

Peggy glared up at Ashley with a frown pushing down eyebrows bushier than Ashley's. She spoke in the kind of raspy voice that said she'd been through a lot in life and most of it wasn't pleasant. "You're taller than I thought."

"You're shorter than I remember."

"Hah!" She gave Ashley a smack on the arm that didn't look painful but didn't look motherly either. "I hear you've been giving that pain in the ass family hell. Good for you." She sat down on the loveseat as relaxed as if they were best friends instead of near strangers.

Ashley avoided the seat next to her mother and sank into the worn cushions of a side chair. "My grandfather has a message for you."

"Iain? How is that old coot doing?"

Peggy didn't even call him Dad. Her attitude was more abrasive than Tori imagined it would be. She glanced at Ashley but couldn't tell how she was taking it.

"He's dying."

Peggy's smile disappeared. "What do you mean dying? He was fit as a fiddle a few months ago."

"I don't know when that was, but he was diagnosed with colon cancer five months ago. It's metastasized into his liver. He's going in for surgery and then staying with Zak for a while."

"Zak." Peggy spat out the name as if it were a swear word. "If the surgery doesn't kill him, staying with Zak will."

Sounded like the same uncle Ashley described.

Ashley spilled out the rest of her message. "He'll be at the Good Samaritan Hospital for three days. He wants you to visit him if you can."

Peggy looked at Tori as if seeing her for the first time. "Who's she?"

Ashley glanced in her direction. "Tori. She's my girlfriend."

"Girlfriend like a friend who's a girl, or like a friend with fringe benefits?"

"Fringe benefits." Ashley stared at Peggy.

Tori joined her in the stare-fest, waiting for the homophobe to come out. That would just be icing on the cake on this visit.

Peggy let out another unpleasant cackle. "You sure are giving them hell, ain't you?"

Peggy wasn't anything like Tori expected. You wouldn't know they were family, other than the physical resemblance. Peggy didn't treat Ashley like a daughter, but she didn't treat her like a stranger either.

Ashley looked like she'd reached her limit. "We have to go. Will you visit your father or not?"

Peggy just shrugged.

"What's that supposed to mean?"

Tori rested her hand on Ashley's shoulder as she bent over to whisper in her ear. "Maybe she can't get there on her own."

Ashley looked at her but Tori just went back to pretending she wasn't intruding in the conversation. Peggy picked imaginary fluff off her faded black pants.

Ashley let out a frustrated sigh. "Do you need money, is that it?"

For the first time, Peggy's eyes flared to life. It wasn't a happy expression. "I've never taken a dime from Iain. I won't start now."

"You get money off Zak and Roy all the time."

"They deserve it. If it wasn't for them, I'd never have left . . ." Peggy glanced at Ashley, then looked away. "I just wouldn't have left. You know what they're like. They drove me out."

"It'll be my turn next," Ashley said.

Peggy sat up. "What do you mean?"

Did Ashley notice the edge in Peggy's voice? Tori wanted to warn her but Ashley kept talking as if she didn't notice the change.

"Come on, Peggy. Put two and two together. You have brain cells left to do that, don't you? *Iain* still supports me. *Iain* is going to Zak's house. Where do you think I'll be living?"

Peggy pulled back as if she'd been slapped. "No. You can't."

Ashley shrugged. "I'll survive."

Peggy grabbed her wrist. "That place is toxic. Find another solution."

What would Zak do to Ashley if she had to live there? Tori's frustrations with her family were miniscule compared to what Ashley's put her through.

"I'm working on it, trust me." Ashley extracted her wrist from Peggy's grasp. Her tone dropped some of its hostility. "You need to work on a way to see my grandfather. It's important to him."

Tori bent down to whisper another suggestion but Ashley's mother interrupted her.

"Just say what you're going to say, Too-tall-for-words. My liver's shot to hell but there's nothing wrong with my hearing."

Tori straightened. "I, um, I was going to say we could drive you down for the visit, if you want."

Ashley stared at Tori as if she'd sprouted a second or maybe even a third head. She'd overstepped her bounds for sure.

Peggy gave Tori a wide grin that exposed a couple of dark gaps where teeth should have been. "I like her. Bring her along when we visit Iain."

It was settled, just that easily. Tori wasn't sure what Ashley would do to her after they got back in the car, but from her expression, it wouldn't be pleasant, and it might just be illegal. Tori wouldn't back out of the offer, though. *You don't let family pass away without saying good-bye*. She knew that better than anyone.

Tori also recognized a spark between Ashley and Peggy that made her think of her own mother. They were as opposite as two people could be, and they showed it in their almost daily battles. Deep down, though, she realized her mother had her back just as much as her father did. It showed in the ways she reacted to Tori's injuries, just the way it showed between Peggy and Ashley when Ashley said she'd have to live with Zak. Ashley needed that protection, even if it came with a package of petty arguments.

Maybe she could teach Ashley the finer points of parental baiting.

Ashley left her cell phone number with Peggy and made plans on when to meet for the hospital visit. Silence reigned on the walk back to the car. Ashley looked tired and more than a little pissed off that Tori had manipulated her into seeing her mother again.

Ashley waited until they were locked in the car before she let loose. "What the hell did I ever do to you to deserve that little stab in the back?"

Tori gripped the steering wheel but wasn't surprised by the outburst. "It won't be that bad. I'll come with you."

"What if I didn't want to see her again?"

"This isn't about you." Tori felt the start of tears in her eyes. "If your grandfather is dying, then she needs to see him before he goes."

Ashley leaned back against the door. "He won't die."

Tori masked wiping her tears with a casual knuckle-rub to the eyes that could have been taking care of an itch. "I didn't see Keisha in the end. The last time she went into the hospital, I refused to go. I didn't know she was never coming back."

The tears that Tori wouldn't shed came as a flood to Ashley. "He can't die. He's the only family I have."

Tori leaned across the car seat to hold her in an awkward hug. She squeezed her eyes shut to hold back her tears. Ashley shook in her arms until her tears stopped.

"Where to now?" Tori asked.

"Home."

TORI WOKE UP to the sound of her cell phone telling her she had a text message waiting. She rolled out of bed and kicked around her dirty clothes until she found the pair of jeans she wore the day before. The phone tumbled out of the back pocket of the jeans, and Tori picked it up to check the message.

Jackie was looking for her.

Tori turned the phone off and tossed it on her bed. Facing the shallowness of her former best friend wasn't on the to-do list for the day. Eating breakfast and getting to college before her one o'clock class was. Her alarm clock said it was almost ten. If the stupid phone hadn't gone off, she could have slept for another hour at least. She scanned the room for a pair of less-dirty pants to put on. The perfect pair sat crumpled beside her bed. With luck, they might even be clean. She put them on, then dug into the pile of t-shirts that lived on the floor in her closet and pulled out a wrinkled shirt with the De Anza logo sprawled across the front.

Everyone else should be gone by now. She made herself a breakfast that would have had the rest of her family clamoring to share it if they were home. She had toast with jam on a side plate. A pair of fried eggs with two strips of bacon stared up at her from a bigger plate. She completed the perfect breakfast with a can of Coke. Her mother would flip at the sheer calories of it all. She picked up her first piece of bacon and took a huge bite.

A knock on the back door stopped her from taking the second bite that would have polished off that strip of bacon. She debated ignoring whoever was at the door. No one else was home, and she wasn't expecting visitors. When the second knock came, she put down the bacon and pushed back her chair. If it was a surprise visit from Ashley, it would be worth letting her breakfast get cold.

Her hopes dimmed when she saw the shadow through the curtains was too short to be Ashley. When she opened the door, her heart sank even further. "Jackie."

Jackie patted her cheek and let herself in. "Something smells good." She walked to the kitchen table and helped herself to Tori's second stripe of bacon.

Tori stood by the door, mourning the loss of her perfect breakfast and wondering how to get rid of Jackie without starting a fight.

Jackie waved her over with her own strip of bacon. "Don't let me stop you. Eat up."

She walked back to the table and grabbed her Coke before Jackie got her hands on that too. "Why are you here?"

"Because you must have lost your phone, again. I sent you a message."

"I know. I read it." She had the satisfaction of watching Jackie freeze on her second bite of the bacon. "You couldn't even face Matt when you broke up with him?"

"I knew you'd take his side. There isn't a good way to break up with someone, you know." Jackie discarded the bacon. "Maybe you'll figure that out when you finally get over Ashley the rebound girl."

"She's not a rebound. I'm in love with her."

Jackie's gaze shifted to the side for an instant and her face paled. "Tori, I'm sorry. I didn't know. I thought you were alone."

Tori was frozen to the spot as Jackie rushed out the door. She held her breath, hoping Jackie was just taunting her. When she heard the telltale sneeze from behind her, she knew she was toast. She turned around and stared into the bloodshot eyes of her mother, who stood in the doorway to the living room, holding a box of tissues in one hand while the other hand was clenched around the front of her fuzzy bathrobe.

The eyes that stared back at her half-disappeared behind the deepest frown Tori had ever seen. "What the hell is going on?"

Truth or evasion, truth or evasion. Tori chose the obvious one. "Nothing."

"Don't get wise with me, Tori Kahl."

How much had her mother overheard? She stuffed her hands in her pockets. "It was nothing, just Jackie being a jerk."

"Are you gay? Is she your girlfriend?"

"What?"

"Don't you lie to me. I don't care if you're an adult, I can still spank your behind. Now tell me the truth."

Tori hadn't been spanked in years but the thought of her mother even trying it now pushed her over the edge. "Fine. Yes. I'm gay. Are you happy now?"

"And Jackie's your girlfriend?"

"No, Jackie's straight. Ashley's my girlfriend."

Tori wasn't sure if her mother was going to cry or scream. Either way, she didn't want to be around for it. The anger that had taken her this far faded and the reality that her life was about to become a living hell took its place. She should have kept her mouth shut. If she hadn't confessed anything, her mother would have no real ammo to come at her for being gay.

That would have been a flat-out lie, though, and she'd never actually lied about her sexuality. She'd been evasive and hidden things, but never openly denied being gay. As she stood there, watching her mother's bowed head, she at least had that to hold onto. When it came down to it, she hadn't denied who she was inside.

Her mother sat down and shook her head. When she looked back up at Tori, her eyes were just as bloodshot as before. Tori couldn't tell if she'd been crying or just building up for a real shouting match. Tori clenched her jaw, waiting for the onslaught.

"Do you do drugs?"

Tori blinked, not sure where that question came from.

"Well, do you?"

"No."

"Steal?"

"No."

"Drink?"

"Not anymore."

Her mother's eyes narrowed at that answer. "But you're gay."

"Yes."

Her mother let out an exasperated sigh. "Well, there are worse sins, I supposed."

"It's not a sin."

"Don't you start with me now, Tori. I just found out my only daughter is gay. I'm in no mood for your games."

She ignored her mother's warning. "So if Keisha were still alive, it would be okay for me to be gay, is that what you're saying?"

"If Keisha were alive you'd have told her first and she could have told me in private. Then you wouldn't be hovering over me waiting for me to make some homophobic slip so you can get all righteous in my face!" Her mother pulled out a tissue and blew her nose so hard Tori thought her own ears would pop in sympathy. "Tori, I'm sorry. You just need to give me some time to think this through."

"I'm gay. What's there to think about?"

"Damn it to hell and back again! You just won't quit, will you? You're my daughter. I love you, and you just drop the biggest secret you probably ever had in my lap. Being gay isn't just about girlfriends and sneaking kisses behind your mother's back, you know. There are people out there who'll hate you for this. You already have people hating you because you're black. Now you have a whole new batch of bigots that'll get in your face and Lord knows what they might do to you some day. You dump all that on me and you think I won't react?"

Tori was too stunned for words. She'd expected her mother to flip, but not this way. She stared down at her bare feet, not sure what to say or how to react. Her mother pushed back out of her chair and walked over to her.

She pulled Tori into a tight hug for a minute, not saying a word, then pushed her away. "You let me tell your father, you hear?"

"Okay."

"What about Jerome, does he know?"

Tori shrugged. "I think so, yeah."

"Hmm. Figures." Her mother sat back down.

Tori shuffled from foot to foot. "I, um, need to get to class."

Her mother waved a hand at her, and Tori took that as her

Sandra Barret

signal that she was free to get the hell out of the house. She rushed upstairs to get her backpack, shoes, and socks. She was back downstairs in less than a minute. Her mother still sat at the table, rolling what Tori hoped was a clean tissue between her fingers. Tori reached across her to retrieve her can of Coke.

Her mother slapped a hand on her wrist. "I want to meet her."

Tori extracted herself, giving up on the soda. "You met her already."

"And it wasn't so favorable, was it? Invite her to dinner. Next week." Tori nodded, and her mother handed her the soda. "You got any other bombs to drop on me?"

"No."

"Good. Now get to class so I can suffer this damned cold in peace."

Tori ran out the door, not sure if she was the luckiest person alive, or if she'd just opened up a whole new level of parental hell by agreeing to bring her girlfriend home for dinner. She hoped Ashley was up to the task.

Chapter 17

"I WANT YOU to come with me to Oakland next Saturday." Tori's mother was on a one-woman mission to remove any doubt Tori had about her heritage. It sucked.

"Yes, Mom. I have to go now." She ducked out of the house before her mother had a chance to bond even more. Is this what Keisha had to put up with on a regular basis? She found a new level of sympathy for her departed sister.

She was short on time, short on patience, and even shorter on luck. Jackie's car pulled into her driveway. She knew what this was about, but she just wanted to get in her car and skip the whole thing. Instead, like the pathetic good person she was becoming, she waited for Jackie to get out and gave a smile she hoped didn't look as fake as it felt.

Jackie stopped two steps from her. "I'm so sorry. I never meant to out you like that."

Tori shrugged. "My parents are okay with it, so I'm kind of glad you did. It makes going out with Ashley easier."

Jackie spread her arms wide. "Still friends?"

"Yeah, sure. Still friends." She accepted Jackie's shallow hug, the perfect match to her own shallow conviction that they'd ever recover the close friendship they used to have. "Sorry, I'm late and Ashley's waiting for me."

"Okay sure. I'll call you, okay?"

"Sure." Jackie gave a little wave before she climbed back into her car. Tori pulled out of the driveway right behind Jackie. What happened to the easy life, when she could come and go without all the well-meaning interruptions?

TORI DROVE ASHLEY along the mountain road that led to her house. She had a surprise for Ashley and so far, Ashley didn't seem to like surprises.

"You said we're not going to your house."

"Right." Tori kept her eyes on the road but her lips curled in a smile. She was having too much fun keeping this secret.

"Because I'm not ready for that dinner with your mother, yet."

"Neither am I. She's getting too nosy with her what's-it-like-to-be-gay questions. Between that and her mission to reintroduce me to her relatives in Oakland, I'm gagging on family bonding time. I'll never complain about not being black enough again."

Ashley shook her head. "And I thought my family was weird."

The road continued to twist and turn. The dry season that turned the valley back to its natural brown state wasn't affecting the Santa Cruz Mountains. Dappled sunlight broke through the canopy of redwoods, pine, and oak that encroached on the roadside.

Ashley leaned forward when they approached Tori's driveway but Tori didn't slow down.

"That was your house, right?"

"Yep."

"Is this another one of your favorite hideaways from home?"

Tori shot her a quick glance. "That depends on you."

Ashley had been trying to get Tori to reveal where they were going for over an hour, but Tori wasn't giving away anything. This really was too much fun.

Ashley wouldn't give up. "I got lost up here, you know. There's not much going on past these next few houses."

"We're almost there." She pulled a sharp turn into what looked like an overgrown deer track into the woods. They bounced along the dried up ruts created by other sets of tires that ventured into this spot in the woods.

"Is this a make out spot?" Ashley asked.

Tori grinned. "I sure hope so."

The trees and brush opened up to a wide patch of hard pack surrounding Matt's tiny A-frame cabin.

Ashley let out a low whistle. "This is for more than just making out. I mean, nice scenery for groping in the backseat, but if you have keys to that cabin, we've got much more interesting possibilities."

Tori dangled another set of keys in front of Ashley. She parked the car and got out.

Ashley stepped out of the car and stretched. "Smells great. Does it always stay like this up here, like the rainy season never stopped?"

"The fog from the ocean rolls in and keeps things from drying out." So far so good. She took Ashley's hand and led her to the cabin. "Come on, there's more."

"You really are anxious to get me naked, aren't you?"

Tori shook her head. "You have a one-track mind sometimes."

"It's a good track."

She unlocked the door and pulled Ashley inside. A sofa, TV, and fireplace identified the living room and a tiny table sat on worn linoleum in the small kitchen. Tori opened up a couple of side doors to point out the bathroom and laundry area, then they climbed up the ladder to the loft.

"There're two bedrooms up here, but this is the important one." She opened up one of the doors, and they squeezed inside a room with a sloped ceiling. The far wall was taken up entirely by a window that looked out through a clearing in the trees. There was a full-sized mattress on the floor, complete with sheets and a quilt that looked like someone's great grandmother made it a century ago. Knowing Matt, it might be his great grandmother's.

Ashley shuffled around the bed to look out the window. "Is that the ocean?"

Tori squeezed in next to her at the window. The treetops rolled down the mountain side until it all disappeared into a tiny spot of bluish-gray. "Yep. An ocean-view room. What do you think?"

Ashley pulled her close, which wasn't difficult in the cramped space. "I think you went through quite a lot to find us a place to make out."

Tori laughed. "It's not just that. Here, maybe this will help." She opened a drawer in the nightstand, pulled out a picture frame, and placed it on the nightstand. It was a photo Michelle had taken of the two of them at the barn. "Look around. It's a place you could call home."

Ashley's eyes widened as she took the room in again. "You mean I can live here?"

"At least through the summer, yes. Maybe longer if you and Matt get along okay."

Ashley's eyes narrowed back down to a frown. "Matt?"

"My friend, remember?" This was the hard part, selling Ashley on living with a stranger. "I guess you haven't met him yet."

"No, I haven't."

"His uncle owns this place. Matt cleaned it all up and moved in a month or so ago."

"I don't know. I may be outgoing, but that doesn't normally include moving in with a strange dude I've never met." Ashley shuffled back out of the room and stood by the loft railing looking down on the tiny living room.

Tori stood next to her. "What's wrong?"

"I'm not sure about all this. I talked to Carmen already, and she'll let me stay with her until the end of the school year."

Shit. Not Carmen again.

"Easy with the jealous glare." Ashley took Tori's hands in hers. "It's not like that and you know it."

"Not anymore."

"Not ever again, either. We crossed that line already, remember? Monogamy." Ashley kissed the tips of Tori's fingers. "I promise, nothing would happen."

Tori relaxed her death-glare. "If you stayed here, nothing would happen for sure."

Ashley returned the smile. "Are you forgetting I'm bi?"

"Oh, yeah."

She laughed and pulled Tori into her arms. "I love you and your little flares of jealousy."

Tori stiffened. Her cheeks heated in an instant. *Did Ashley mean that?*

"Did I say something wrong?"

"You love me?" She held Ashley's gaze in hers, waiting.

Ashley blushed. "Yes, I mean it."

"I love you, too." She planted feather-light kisses on Ashley's cheeks, forehead, and lips. Her touch was so light that it didn't ignite the passion she usually felt for Ashley, but it spread a different kind of warmth through her that she hadn't felt before.

Ashley led them back into the bedroom. "When do I get to meet this Matt person?"

"He's staying at his parents' house tonight." Tori felt nervous all of a sudden.

"So you planned this all out, did you?"

"No, I didn't."

Ashley smiled. "Really, because if you weren't planning on something, I'd be disappointed."

Tori blushed. "Well, I wouldn't want to disappoint you."

Ashley grinned. "Are you sure?"

Tori put her fingers on Ashley's lips. "We can take it slow."

Tori replaced her fingers with her lips in a kiss that left them both breathless.

"Slow is good," Ashley said when she regained the ability for speech.

WHEN TORI WOKE up the first time, the moon illuminated the tiny room, casting everything in shades of gray and shadow. She tried to roll away from the moonlight, but Ashley wrapped herself even closer. She used her free arm instead to cover her eyes and drifted back off to sleep.

The next time Tori woke up, the patch of sky visible from the bedroom window was showing the burnt orange of sunrise. She shut her eyes again, but couldn't ignore the call of nature that had woken her up. She slipped out of bed in her ruffled t-shirt and boxers. Ashley frowned in her sleep and curled around Tori's pillow.

She sat for a few minutes, just watching Ashley sleep. She was beautiful, not in the traditional sense, but in a way that made her heart ache as she watched. There was no sign of the play-it-cool attitude Ashley presented when she was awake, nor any of the vulnerability she'd let Tori see in the last few days. Asleep, Ashley was at peace. Tori wished she could capture and keep this moment for always.

Ashley rolled the other way and ducked under the quilt. Tori took that as her cue and padded out of the room to the bathroom downstairs. She wasn't sleepy anymore so instead of disturbing Ashley's sleep, she stepped outside and sat on the back porch. The sun rose over the treetops. The air was crisp, with an early morning dampness that would disappear soon.

"What are you doing out here?" Ashley stood in the doorway, wrapped in the quilt. She had one eye shut, as if signifying half of her was still asleep.

"Sorry, I didn't want to wake you up."

"My cell phone did that anyway. My mother bought one of those pay as you go cell phones. I'll be picking her up tomorrow to visit my grandfather."

"Are you okay?"

Ashley looked off at the trees for a minute. "Yeah, I think so. I'm not ready for him to die, but I know it's going to happen sooner or later, isn't it?"

Tori closed her eyes, remembering how Keisha faded at the end. It all happened so quickly, too quickly for her to deal with at the time. Robyn was useless to talk to, so wrapped up in her own world to see what Tori was going through. She wouldn't let that happen to Ashley. Almost a year after Keisha's death, she was ready to accept that loss, and let that experience help Ashley cope in the coming months.

For now, though, she knew Ashley needed to think about something else. "Do you want me to come with you to get your mother?"

Ashley smiled. "Thanks, but I'll be okay. If you're there, I know I'll just hide behind you and not make an effort to get to know her, you know?"

She'd rather be there with Ashley, but she couldn't force herself into the situation. "Don't let her hurt you again."

"Becoming overprotective already? That's sweet but don't worry. All I'm hoping for is that we can be civil. Maybe act like we're related instead of total strangers."

"Okay."

"I did tell her I won't have to go live with Zak. That made her happy."

Tori's eyes widened. "You mean you'll move in here?"

"At least through the summer, maybe longer if Matt's not a freak."

Tori didn't mention that he was kind of a freak, but in a good way. Ashley would figure that out for herself soon enough. "We'll be neighbors." She'd be close by, when Ashley needed her.

"Yeah, I guess a mile away qualifies as neighbors up here." Ashley shuffled over and draped the quilt around Tori. "It's cold out here."

"It's not that bad."

Ashley kissed her on the tip of the nose. "Yes, it is. Come back to bed."

She smiled. "Is that an invitation?"

"To sleep, yes." Ashley rested her head on Tori's shoulder.

Tori grinned. She knew Ashley was still half asleep. "Come on, sleepy. Back to bed."

Ashley managed to drag herself back up the ladder without losing her quilt, a talent Tori didn't think she possessed herself. She followed Ashley into the bedroom and crawled back under the covers. The window had no blinds, so the light of morning filled the room. That didn't bother Ashley, who was already breathing in a slow, steady rhythm. She curled herself around Ashley and stared at the picture she'd put on the night-stand. The two of them were sitting on the picnic table, Ashley wrapped in Tori's arms and both smiling into the camera. It was the first picture taken of them as a couple.

So much had happened in the past year. A lot of it was bad. Some of it was painful to even think about. The shining light in all of it was Ashley and what they had together now. She closed her eyes. As she drifted off to sleep, she wondered what Keisha would have thought of Ashley. She'd have liked her. They'd have liked each other.

ABOUT THE AUTHOR

This is where an author would normally include her biography. In place of that, Sandra included the following four tidbits about herself. Three are flat-out lies, one is a true:

- She was arrested as a teenager, but her police officer uncle got her off with a warning.

- She is terrified of balloons. Terrified.

- Spiders on the other hand, are a-okay after she ate one on a dare in the sixth grade.

- She paddles her kayak in the sheep pasture when it floods.

Email her at sbarret_fic@yahoo.com with your guess on which one is true, or visit her website at http://www.sandrabarret.com for a more traditional bio.